HUBRIS

THE CHARITY DEACON INVESTIGATIONS BOOK 1

P.A. WILSON

FREE EBOOK

Claim your copy of Buying Into Death when you use the QR code to sign up for my newsletter and follow Charity as she solves her fastest case yet!

ONE

I'm a P.I. I know that sounds cool and dangerous, but mostly it's just seedy. Every now and then I feel like chucking it all in, but then someone asks for my help, and I get back in the groove. When I'm in the groove, I follow wandering spouses, dig into employees' finances, and occasionally track down a missing person.

When I'm not doing the PI thing, I do a little journalism. I've also waited tables, driven a tour bus, and put in a few shifts at a retail store. That's me, Charity Deacon, five foot eight inches of black haired, blue eyed, Renaissance woman.

I was sitting on the patio of the Starbucks on the corner of Robson and Thurlow. It was fall and the pumpkin lattes were in season. Just as I started to zone out, a screeching crash broke the mood.

The noise came from a white Jeep bouncing off the back of a bus across Thurlow. I dropped my latte and grabbed my camera, clicking pictures as I ran.

Sirens wailed closer.

I could see that the bus was empty. Out of the corner of my eye, I saw the driver running from the Starbucks across the intersection – yes there are two – carrying a coffee in one hand, and pulling his mobile phone out of his pocket with the other. He threw the coffee in the middle of the street when it got in the way of dialing.

As I reached the Jeep, a police car pulled up. One of the cops jumped out and ran to yank open the driver's door. A body fell sideways and hung from the seatbelt. I could tell it was a body, and no longer a person, because it flopped and there was white powder from the airbag all over its face. The powder stained red from the blood oozing from the hole just below his ear.

I took pictures then ran around to the other side before the police could stop me. The passenger door opened, and a man stumbled out before folding at the knees, and planting his face on the asphalt. I kept snapping for a dozen more shots and then focused on the street action.

"Miss, please step back." One of the cops walked into my camera range, a blurry flesh colored barrier between the action and me.

I obeyed. Well, technically the small step I took was back. Switching to video mode, I started panning the crowd. The cop put his hand in front of the lens.

"Step farther back," he said.

I tried not to sigh. I knew from my history with the cops, it would just antagonize him. "I'm not in the way. I'm not interfering. What's the problem?"

"Can I get your name and address, please?"

"Why?"

"You were a witness." The cop looked at my camera. It felt like a threat. Maybe that was because I'd been threatened by the cops before. They didn't like it when people pointed out their failings.

I reminded myself to keep my tone even. "That doesn't mean I can't take pictures."

The cop sighed. "Look, you can give me your details now, and I'll let you take the pictures while we get the other statements. Or, you can wait over there until we get around to taking your statement and you lose your photo op. Your choice."

"Fine. Charity Deacon, number 9 Dock B, 1525 Coal Harbour Quay, 604 555 5555."

He wrote it down, and then I went back to videoing the bystanders.

"Don't go anywhere without giving us your statement."

I ignored him and swept my camera over the gathering crowd, recording the cop's head as he walked across my line of sight. "Asshole," I muttered.

I shot a video of the people on the sidewalk, mostly people trying to see and not see at the same time. Turning, I scanned across the street. A few cars were backed up at the intersection, but one in particular caught my attention. Two men stood beside a black SUV, both well dressed and well built. What made them stand out were the smiles they wore; identical and smug.

I swung the camera past to get a panorama before checking the battery level, almost out. I flicked back to photo and snapped pictures of as many people as I could. The two men climbed back into their vehicle and drove away as I took the last few shots.

When I got back to the Starbucks patio, the bus driver was talking to one of the constables. "I'll get fired for this," he moaned. "I'm not supposed to stop there."

"Look at it this way," the cop answered. "If the bus wasn't there to stop the Jeep, we'd be carting a few more bodies to the morgue, and a lot more to the ER."

I made a mental note to call Transit and commend the

actions of the bus driver. The cop was right, and the guy shouldn't get shit for taking a quick break.

There were three other uniformed cops taking statements from the twenty or so people who had stopped to see what was going on.

While I waited, I had some time so I tried to add a little to my bottom line with my photos. I made some calls, the Vancouver Sun and Province, the Courier, and the local TV news station. The newspapers told me they would take my pictures if I could send the files by the evening deadline, but the TV station already got their footage from someone else.

TWO

That same afternoon, my best friend Lu and I sat on the rooftop patio of my floating home in Coal Harbour, enjoying a bottle of Malbec and a plate of nibbles.

The marina was quiet. Most of the boats that surrounded our small community of houses were docked and deserted. There were a few seagulls circling for scraps, but they weren't screaming.

I liked the contrast between the peace of the marina, and the bustle of the community outside the gate.

Lu and I had been friends since the first day of kindergarten when I'd run onto the playground at recess looking forward to playing. Instead of the swings my eyes focused on four of the biggest kids surrounding this tiny Asian girl who was standing with her fists clenched and face red, clearly trying not to cry. I stomped over, shoved two of the bullies out of my way, and stood next to her with my fists raised.

Since then, we've stood side by side through every important event: her wedding, and then her husband's funeral five years later, my first real relationship, from passionate start to disastrous end, and my parent's memorial service.

She played with the four heavy gold bands circling her wrist. "If you think those men were up to something, why didn't you call the cops and tell them what you saw?"

"I didn't know it was anything." I held up the bottle, but Lu shook her head, so I poured the remainder into my glass. "I mean, it looked suspicious, but maybe they were just checking to see if there was anything they could do?"

"You don't sound like you believe that." Lu raised an eyebrow. "You said they looked proud."

I hate it when she's got a point. "You know, the cops don't like me right now. What would I have said to them anyway?"

Lu twitched her mouth in a smile. "How about something like, I think those two men might have had something to do with this. Charity, your job isn't to prove anything. It's to point out something you think might be important."

I had hoped for some encouragement, but Lu was right. I should probably have told the cops, even though some of them are still pretty ticked at me. It's not my fault one of their own was beating his wife, and I found out. Although, I guess they might have reason to blame me for going to the press. "Well, actually, my job is to investigate cases for my clients."

"True." Lu checked her watch. "You keep telling me that, but you also keep telling me you are tired of investigating people's problems. If you don't commit to this, you'll never get better at it."

I couldn't argue with that. "I know, I know. I just feel like I need to do more important stuff than taking pictures of cheating spouses."

She laughed and flicked at a mosquito. "Then you need to get better at it, so you can get better cases."

"Yeah, we can talk about that later. Right now, I'm making enough money to do what I need, so let's leave it."

"But I know you've forgone the pay part of it a couple of times."

"I can afford to do some pro bono work." I thought that sounded much more professional than free. "It's only when I think the job will be easy."

"I know, but you aren't always right." Lu swallowed the last drop of wine in her glass. "I've given up trying to talk you out of that stuff. I was just making an observation. In fact, what does Mike think about your adventures in pro bono?"

Mike was my uncle, and my only living relative. I hadn't mentioned today's events to him, yet. "Nothing. He helps me with connections, but he doesn't feel the need to comment."

"Sure." Lu laughed. "It must be helpful to have connections in the – what? Spy world? Oh yeah, he's a security consultant. Speaking of connections, send me some pictures, and I will see if I can get anything for you."

"I thought it was too dangerous."

"It is but I'll be discreet."

"Well, I'll check the pictures and video more carefully tonight," I said. "I'll talk to the cops tomorrow if I can find anything more than just suspicion."

"Good." Lu looked over at my neighbor's roof. "Is Jake still working on that series about the mayor?"

Before I could answer, I heard the doorbell ring, then a rapid knocking, and a "hey are you home?"

"Shit, that's all I need. You know Delores is going to tear me a new one for the noise." I ran through the bedroom and downstairs.

I pulled the door open to see a skinny Asian girl dressed in a black miniskirt, torn fishnet stockings, cropped tee shirt, and piercings in lips, eyebrow, and nose.

"Jeez, how did you get through the security gate?" I looked

down toward Delores Markham's house. Relieved that no one was peering through the curtains. "Who are you? What do you want?"

"Nice way to welcome a client, bitch." The girl looked like a child and carried herself like a biker. "An old guy let me in."

Most of my neighbors were pretty careful about the security gate. "Did he know he let you in?"

"Maybe not." The girl shrugged. "You going to let me in? I got a job for you."

I checked her out and decided that between Lu and I, we were probably safe from any trouble this kid could cause. I stepped aside to let her into the living room. "What's your name?"

"Val."

"Val what?"

"Just Val."

"How did you know where I lived?" I saw Lu peek around the corner of the stairs and nodded her to stay up there.

"A guy told me." Val looked around the small room. I hoped she wasn't casing the joint. "So, you ask all your clients this many questions?"

"I usually don't meet people in my home." I kept my client meetings at coffee shops. It was easier than trying to dodge impatient ones on the wharf. "Would you like a soda?"

"A beer would be better."

"I'm pretty sure you aren't old enough." I passed Val a diet Coke and pointed to the dining area. Pulling out a pad of paper from the backpack I'd left hanging on the back of my chair, I asked, "How old are you anyway?"

"I'm eighteen."

I raised an eyebrow.

"Okay, I'm sixteen. You find people, right?" She turned the can around clicking her black painted nails on the side.

"I take missing persons cases, yes. Who's missing?" I couldn't figure out why she was being so aggressive when she wanted me to help.

"The guy said you were good." Val continued to play with the can. Looking closer, I could see a bruise under the thick makeup on her face. I saw another, older bruise showing on her arm.

No needle marks, which I took as a good sign.

"Where do you live?"

She didn't answer.

"Can you tell me where you live?" This was getting tired. If she didn't start answering questions, I wouldn't be able to help her.

"Why, you got some kind of residency requirement?" Val started to bounce on the ball of her right foot as though she was getting ready to run. The movement caused her entire body to shake, but she seemed oblivious to it.

I put my pen down and took the can from Val. "Look, you came to me. You banged on my door like the devil was after you. Tell me what you want or get out. I have things to do."

"Okay, chill. I need to know how much it will cost." She reached into her pocket and pulled out a wad of bills. "I can put this down now and get you more later... when you find her."

"Where did you get the money from?" I thought I knew what Val was going to say.

"You think my money is dirty? Look, I earned this." She pushed the bills toward me. "I didn't steal it."

I ignored the money. "Tell me who's missing."

Val forced her lips together and swallowed before speaking. "My sister, she disappeared."

The shell was cracking, and I saw the scared child inside. "Where are your parents?"

"Turning to worm food." Val's casual shrug didn't match with the catch in her voice. "It's only Emma and me."

"I'm sorry." I remembered how alone I'd felt when my parents had died in India. That was the hardest call I had ever had to take. "What did the police say?"

"Hah. You think the cops are interested in looking for a hooker. They got Picton and now it's like they think no other hookers count."

Despite the bravado, I could hear pain in the tightness of her voice. "That's not true and I think you know it. Did you go to the police?"

"No." Val looked down at her lap. "I don't want to get them involved."

Lots of my clients don't want the police involved. But, this time, that wouldn't work. I needed them to start a missing person's file. "Fine, where are you living?"

"I got a place, don't worry. What about my sister?"

Okay, I was done with this dancing around. If I couldn't get an answer to my questions, I'd see if she could do as I asked. "I don't like taking a case that should be with the police. I need you to go report her missing. Come back with a case number, and I'll think about it."

Val stopped bouncing her foot and looked up. "Only think about it?"

"That's all I'll promise." I wasn't sure I wanted to get involved, but I didn't want to say no now that she'd pulled in her thorns.

"Okay." Val sighed. "I'll do it now and come right back."

"No. Just phone, give me the case number, and tell me what the police say." I needed to get back to those pictures and I hoped the cops would solve her problem.

"Fine. If you don't want to help me, you should just say so."

Val stared at the money on the table. "Is it because of the money? It's not dirty, you know."

"It's not the money." I felt sorry for her. The thorns were back out, but she seemed to be wearing an armor made of attitude, one I'd seen on a lot of street kids. She was still a kid, and by the way she swallowed before talking about her sister, a scared kid. "Look. I think the police will investigate, but give me some information now, and I'll see what I can find out. What's her name?"

"Emma."

I almost told her to forget it. If I was going to have to drag every bit of information out of her, it was going to be an uphill battle. But she was so young under that attitude, I couldn't do it. "I need a last name. I can't find someone by just a first name."

"Wei. Our last name is Wei."

"That wasn't so hard, was it? When did she disappear?"

"The last time I saw her was two days ago. She was going out to start work."

"What does she do?"

"She's a hooker. So what?" Her eyes shone, chin jutted.

"Val, I need to know where to start looking."

"Oh, okay. She works down on the Eastside, and sometimes around The Drive."

"What does she look like? Do you have a picture?"

"No. No pictures. She's a bit taller than me."

Val was at least four inches shorter than me. "So, five five, or six?"

"Uh huh. Her hair has red streaks in it, and it's cut short and spiky."

"Okay, any tats or piercings?"

"Yep. A butterfly on her ass."

Was she trying to be deliberately obstructive? "Val, stop fighting me on this. If you can't just answer my questions, I can't help you. Now, anything I might see when she has her clothes on?" I heard the annoyance snap in my voice. *Calm and professional.*

Val shook her head. "She tried to look straight. We were going to get off the street. She didn't want to mark herself as a hooker."

"What was she wearing the last time you saw her?" I kept scratching notes on the pad, trying not to look at Val, trying not to antagonize her.

"Jeans, a white wife beater and red stilettos."

"Who is her pimp?"

"No pimp. We look after each other."

"Okay." I flipped the pages back and pulled out a business card. "You go talk to the cops, and call me at this number when you're done."

Val looked at the card, turned it over and back. "Charity Deacon Investigations. Sounds very official." She sniffed.

"It is." I stood and pointed to the door. "The sooner you get to the police station, the better."

"Fine, I can take a hint." Val jerked up from the chair. "I'll call you as soon as I'm done with the cops."

I escorted her to the security gate and pulled it tight when she walked away. Val burst out laughing then strode off.

Lu was watching from the patio when I ran back to the house. "Hey, I thought you were focusing on the case from this afternoon."

"Hush, the neighbors don't need to know everything that's going on." I shut the door and grabbed a bottle of white wine from the fridge before going upstairs.

Lu pushed her glass toward me. "I heard everything. What are you going to do?"

"Hope the police will take the case seriously." I didn't think they would do much but hoping doesn't take any effort.

Lu shook her head. "I'm sure they will, but taking it seriously, and finding a missing person isn't the same thing."

"Well, I'll ask around a bit and help her out. It can't hurt." I poured wine into our glasses.

Lu picked up hers and I heard her mutter, "I'm sure it can," before taking a sip.

THREE

After Lu left, I went down to my office, booted up my laptop, and started a file for Val's case. Missing person cases were either very easy, or absolutely impossible. The easy ones usually involved adults running away from their responsibilities. They didn't always do a great job of covering up their trail. The impossible ones were about kids running away from home to the streets. Or as in Val's case, street people disappearing. I'd need a lot of help from Val on who to talk to. I didn't have many contacts in the Downtown Eastside life.

When a prostitute went missing, the reason fell into two general categories: women who find a way out of the life and don't want to be found and, like so many of the women on the Downtown Eastside, women killed by the sex trade. Death too easily came at the hand of a john, or on the point of a needle. The problem was I couldn't think of any easy answers to one very important question. If Emma had left the life, why hadn't she taken Val?

After transferring my notes from paper into a Word document, I added a list of places to start the search, names of two cops I knew who might have heard something and won't be too mad at me, and the name of a social worker who would help Val if I could get them together.

"Nothing else to do until she calls." I closed the file and put my notes into the shredder.

I needed some tea. While I waited for the water to boil I looked out the living room window to Jake's house. He lives next-door waterside. We have a casual relationship, not really open, not really committed, definitely hot. I liked it that way, but lately he was acting like he wanted more.

He was still out. Maybe later.

Taking the steaming mug with me, I opened the folder where I'd uploaded the pictures and video of the accident. I ran a slide show, seeing anonymous faces flick by and vehicles stopped by the obstruction. While I looked through, I ran the face recognition program to group faces, maybe something would show up in an expression.

"Okay, what are you looking for?" I couldn't define or dismiss the feeling that there was something I could get my hands on, something that would be useful.

I ran the video and watched as people reacted to the sight of blood and bodies. As the scene panned to the corner across from the accident, I saw the black SUV and the two men standing beside it. Lu was right. I need to pass this information on to the police. As soon as I figure out exactly what information I had, I would.

I stopped the video and zoomed in on the license plate of their vehicle, making a note of the number. I ran the rest of the video and watched them get back into the SUV and pull away.

"Damn, how does this work again?" I muttered, looking for a hint about how to print a frame from a video. Running the video back to the frame that showed the best picture of the two men, I clicked the help button, searched for the print help, and then printed the frame to a PDF file. I really should make sure I figure out how to use the stuff I buy.

I created a folder for the accident, copied the pictures and video into it, and then printed everything out, placing it in a paper file for back up. The phone interrupted me just as I started making notes.

"Deacon Investigations."

"Yo, Charity,"

"Hi, Val, do you have a case number?"

Val sighed as though the weight of the world sat on her shoulders. "It took forever."

I didn't buy into the dramatics. "At this time of night, there aren't a lot of people on shift at the station. But they did listen?"

"Yeah, you were right, they listened. I don't think they'll do anything, but they listened." Val gave me the case number.

"Okay, how do I get hold of you?"

"What do you mean? I'm there tomorrow morning. We're going to find my sister."

"Not we." I didn't need to worry about what Val would do while I asked questions.

"Yes, we. I'm coming. You can't stop me."

I reminded myself that I was the adult, and didn't react to her tone. I needed her help after all, but I had planned to interview her and then go looking for Emma. "I would prefer to do this alone."

"Yeah, well, I prefer to come along. How are you planning to stop me?"

I realized there was no winning this argument. Teenagers seem to have an endless supply of attitude. "Okay, you can come, as long as you agree that you do as I say. If not, I just hand off the case to the cops. Agreed?"

"Agreed. Just don't tell me to do anything stupid like stay away from the streets."

I thought she agreed too quickly, but I let it go for now. "Deal. We can talk tomorrow about how to get started."

"Tomorrow? Why not now?"

"I'm tired, and we don't have a plan."

"Shit, we can't wait. She could be in major trouble." Val's voice cracked. I heard panic start to build.

"No. The cops are on it." I tried to sound reassuring. "We need to have a plan, not just go jumping in all energy and no focus."

"But..."

"No, but. Spend the time thinking about what you remember from the last time you saw her."

"Fine, I'll be there tomorrow, early." She hung up.

"What does early mean to a teenage hooker?"

Stop talking to yourself. I wondered if telling myself to stop talking was a sign I was already beyond hope.

I'd lost my inspiration, so I shut down the laptop and put the empty mug in the sink. I wasn't ready to sleep, but a glance over to Jake's house showed that he was still not home. I grabbed my phone and pressed the speed dial button for his mobile. "Hey, where are you?"

"On my way down from the parking lot. Should I stop at your place?"

I opened the door and saw Jake heading down the gangway. "Brilliant idea, baby. I missed you."

He chuckled. "I've been away for two days, crazy stalker. Thanks for missing me."

JAKE PRODDED ME. "FOOD, PLEASE."

"What time is it?" I rolled away from his warm body and reached for the alarm clock. "Is it tomorrow yet?"

"Yes, it's tomorrow." Jake poked me again. "You just don't recognize the time of day. It's five am. I'm due on set at seven."

"And you want food?" I rubbed my face. Jake was right, this definitely was not my usual nine o'clock daybreak.

"Not *only* food. But I need sustenance before I tend to my other wants." He gave me a gentle shove. "Food, woman."

"Well, only because you were so good last night." Grabbing my robe from the chair, I started downstairs. "Tea and toast okay?"

I heard him laugh. "If I say no?"

"Yeah, it wasn't really a question," I called back up to him.

I dropped bread in the toaster and put the kettle on to boil. "Crap, I should really keep groceries in the house for these kinds of situations."

"What?" Jake called.

"Talking to me, not you." You would think he'd remember I talked to myself. Come to think of it, you'd think I would remember he was here.

I sniffed the milk before pouring it into a jug, looked for jam and found honey instead. I spread butter on the toast, poured water into the teapot, and went back up to the bedroom.

"Changed my mind." Jake took the tray and put it on the floor. "Come here."

He slipped the robe off my shoulders and ran his hands down my back. I could feel the warmth of his breath as his lips brushed the nape of my neck. It tickled my skin, the tingling slid down my spine and I pressed into him as he reached around to slide his hands over my stomach.

The tingle increased as his hand slid lower. Impatient, I turned in his embrace to arch against him. I fell backward, pulling him down onto the bed.

· · ·

AFTER A HOT HALF HOUR, we sat in bed eating cold, soggy toast and drinking fresh tea. I sighed and tried to curl up under the covers to go back to sleep.

"Can you put on the news?" Jake asked. "I need to know the traffic situation. We're filming at Britannia mine this morning."

"Sure, maybe I'll even get up when you go." I dug around until I found the remote under the duvet that lay piled on the floor beside the bed.

"...thanks, Donald," the newscaster said, her smile turning serious as a photograph of a suburban house flicked onto the screen behind her. "Police report another home invasion late yesterday. Mrs. Yeung was killed in the family home. Her two children witnessed the brutal murder which came only a few hours after her husband died in a car accident in downtown Vancouver."

"Shit, that's gotta be the crash I saw." I leaped out of bed and pointed to the screen. "I knew there was more to it."

"What are you talking about?" Jake pulled on his clothes as he spoke.

"I saw the crash. The wife being killed the same day isn't just a coincidence. It can't be. I'm going to figure out what's really going on." *Those two guys had something to do with it, or I'm totally in the wrong business.*

"Who's the client?"

Oops. "No client, yet." I ignored the look Jake shot at me. "I have another case starting today."

He pulled me close and murmured into my hair "I don't want you to get involved with anything this dangerous, with or without a client."

"Good thing you're not the boss of me." I could feel my defenses thud into place. Our warm morning glow extinguished, I pushed him away making an effort to do it gently.

He stood up and grabbed his shoes. "I'm not trying to

control you, Charity. Jeez, you always overreact. I'm just saying, if you're right and it's not a coincidence, then it's going to be nasty and dirty. You don't want to step into that kind of mess. A whole family has been slaughtered for Christ's sake." He stamped his feet into his shoes.

My cheeks started to burn, and I did my best to keep the anger in check. "I don't know how messy it is, and I don't know if I can even find anything to work with. But I don't want to let this go." I saw the look he gave me and cooled off a bit. "I won't take too many chances, I promise." I wanted to avoid arguing with Jake when he had to leave, and we wouldn't have time to finish it. Unresolved fights leave me with heartburn.

"Okay. If you promise to be careful, I'll try not to tell you to be safe." Jake grabbed me around the waist and gave me a long, deep, goodbye kiss.

Heartburn avoided.

FOUR

"Hey, where are you?" Val called out as she walked into my living room a half hour later.

I stopped drying dishes and looked out through the doorway of the kitchen. "How did you get through the gate? And, don't just walk in, at least knock."

"Chill, the gate isn't that hard to get through." Val hung her leather jacket over the back of a chair. "Maybe I did knock. Maybe you didn't hear it."

She was back in tough chick mode. "No. you didn't knock." I realized this was becoming a familiar argument and waved my hands to stop it. "Doesn't matter." I picked up my notepad and pointed Val to the chair. *Time to get something I could work with.*

"Yeah. Before you get started we need to talk money." Val stood with her hands jammed in the pockets of her shorts. Today she was dressed in high black boots, very short black pants, and a white tank. "I'm not a charity case. Hah. Get it? Charity case."

"Yeah, I never heard that before." While I waited for her to continue, I mentally chanted a mantra, *don't react, be patient.*

"I guess." Val pulled a roll of money from her pocket. "Look, I have two hundred dollars here." She put the money on the table. "How much of your time will that buy?"

"Not much." I looked at her. A scared kid looked back through the bravado. I could afford to do this for free because my parents had left me enough to be comfortable, although not wealthy. "I don't need your money. I'll help find Emma, don't worry. You can do some of the work to minimize the cost."

"Damn right I'll help. I'm not going to sit here, and wait for you to get back to me. I expect a discount on your rate, but I'm paying."

I picked up the wad of bills, mostly tens. Users paid for drugs that way. Did johns pay the same way? "Where did you get this?"

"Where do you think?"

"Prostitution?" I hoped she'd say she won the lottery — I'm an optimist.

"No! I figured you'd have a problem with that. You being a solid citizen, and all."

Don't argue, be patient. "Selling drugs?"

"No! Crap you don't think much of me, do you?"

That brought on a twinge of guilt. She had a point. "So where did you get it? You're right, I won't take dirty money."

Val looked out the window before she answered. I could see the moisture at the corner of her eyes. "I sold something. It was mine to sell. Don't worry, I didn't steal it, and it wasn't my body."

I figured that was the best I was going to get. "Okay, I'll take it. If you work with me then the money will last a long time." I didn't want to talk about how long right now.

"You'll let me know when you need more? I'll figure something out so you won't soil your hands with my earnings." Val had sucked her lower lip between her teeth.

"Leave that for when we need to talk about it." I looked at her again. "Have you eaten breakfast?"

"No, I don't usually eat this early. Let's get started."

"Well, today you are going to eat breakfast. You need to keep your strength up to find your sister. Come on, we'll go out and get something to eat while we get the plan worked out. My treat."

"I can buy my own breakfast." Val seemed determined not to take anything she hadn't earned. I wondered why I thought that was odd.

"Think of it as a breakfast meeting. I'm hungry and I said it's my treat." I handed Val her jacket, grabbed my keys and backpack then started toward the door.

"Okay, take a chill pill. Are you going to be this bossy all the time?"

"Probably," I said, locking the door behind us.

We walked along the quay toward the Bayshore. I love the walk to the hotel. Today, the sun gave off more light than warmth, the way it usually does in September. If you ignored the slight tinge of diesel in the air, and focused on the sights of boats in the marina and the mountains across the inlet, you feel like you are in heaven.

"How can you live down here?" Val asked pointing to the wall of buildings on the west side of the quay.

"I like being down by the park." I nodded toward Stanley Park to the right. "I can walk on the seawall, or go shopping." Okay, shopping was ten blocks away, but I could walk there.

She stopped. "Wow. Do you walk all the way around the park?"

"No, I said I could." I didn't think the small talk was taking the edge off Val's fear for her sister, but it was better than watching her vibrate.

"I think there's probably too many tourists for me." She

shrugged. "At least too many of the kind of tourist that don't need my services."

Maybe time to get some background. "Val, how did you and Emma end up in the Downtown Eastside?"

"You don't think we grew up there?" She moved away from me and walked along the edge near the water.

"No." I couldn't explain exactly why, but she didn't seem hard enough to have grown up there. The whole street attitude seemed more like an act than anything else.

"We didn't." She ran across the small raised lawn in front of the Starbucks and pulled the door open. I took the hint and put my personal questions on the back burner.

I pointed to the stack of English muffins in the food case. "What do you want to eat, one of those breakfast sandwiches?"

"A pumpkin latte with extra cream and a cupcake." Val lounged against the counter. "A chocolate cupcake."

Oh, yeah that sounded like a nice nutritious breakfast.

"A pumpkin latte, extra cream, a shot in the dark, and two bacon sandwiches," I told the scrawny young man behind the counter.

Val frowned. "What are you my grandmother? I want the cupcake."

"I'll stop acting like a grandmother, when you stop acting like a two-year-old. Cupcakes are not for breakfast. They are dessert."

"So, can I have one after I eat the sandwich?" Val asked.

"Duh." I poked her arm. "Dessert is what comes after the meal, right." As long as she had some protein in her stomach, a cupcake couldn't hurt.

"Oh." Val managed a quick smile, one that didn't remove the worry from her eyes. "I take back the grandmother bit."

We took the food to a small table in the window facing the Marina. I handed Val some napkins and pulled out my notepad.

Holding the sandwich in one hand and a pen in the other, I asked, "Okay, where have you looked already?"

"In her usual stroll, Downtown Eastside and along Hastings around Commercial," she answered around a mouthful of food. "I asked some of the girls working on the streets. No one has seen her for a couple of days. They don't remember when it was, or who she was with. It's like she just disappeared."

I imagined how Val had asked people — interrogated them more likely. "It's all in how you ask. Don't worry, we'll go back there, and I'll ask the questions." I took a sip of my coffee. It complemented the greasy, salty sandwich the way red wine enhanced blue cheese. "What did you tell the police?"

"That she's missing and they should find her." Val stuck her tongue in the pile of whipped cream that was floating on the latte.

"What did they say?" I resisted the urge to wipe cream from Val's nose, reminding myself that she wasn't a child. She was sixteen and more experienced than I was in the harsher realities of adult life.

"They asked, like, who did she hang out with, did she have any regulars, did she do this before? Disappear, like."

This was going to be painful if I was going to drag information from her. I picked up the wrappers from the sandwiches and went to the counter to purchase the cupcakes.

"So, it sounds like they are taking this seriously," I said, holding out the two brightly iced cakes for her to choose.

Val took the chocolate one, and swiped her finger through the pile of icing, licking it off before speaking. "I guess. So, when are we going to start the investigation? When do we start taking names and kicking asses?"

I understood Val's need to start the investigation immediately. After all, her sister was her only family. "We need a plan first. So, if we have to kick asses, we'll kick the right ones." I checked my coffee, hoping to see another sip at the bottom of the mug. "Where are you staying? I might need to get in touch with you."

"There's no phone there, I'll get in touch with you." Val looked out at the pedestrians passing. "We should have a schedule. You know, I come by at nine every morning? That way you don't need to worry about getting in touch."

"I'd feel much better if I knew I could reach you." I suspected that Val was living in some squat, or on the street. "If I know you are okay, I can think better, and that will help find your sister faster."

"No problem, I'll get a phone. You can call me." Val kept her eyes on the street. "So, are we going to start looking for her now?" The words came out plaintively, the sixteen-year-old child surfacing though the hardness of the streetwalker.

I sighed, knowing no one would be up at this time in the morning to answer our questions. "I have some stuff I need to do first. Unless you know someone we can talk to at this time in the morning. We can't start until tonight."

Val opened her mouth to argue, and then thought it over. "Yeah, you're right. Everyone will be sleeping off last night, or doing special orders."

Good, now for some information. "So, do you have any names for me?"

Val wiped her fingers on her shorts and then pulled a crumpled paper from her pocket. "I wrote this list of names last night."

I looked at it, about twenty names written in a beautiful hand. "These are all women. What about men, clients."

"I only know a few first names." Val shrugged. "They're probably not real names, anyway."

I didn't argue. Men who frequented prostitutes, particularly young prostitutes, would not be broadcasting their identities. "Well, can you give me some descriptions of her regulars?"

"No. I was too busy with my clients to pay any attention to hers. How do you usually find missing people?"

"I find people who knew them and ask questions. I try to find out if they've used an ATM or their Visa."

"You can do that?" I heard a faint ring of respect in her voice, and hoped she'd start trusting me to do the job.

"Yes. But I'm not supposed to be able to do it, so don't tell anyone."

"No prob. I don't think Emma has a Visa or ATM card."

I saw Val's leg start to shake again, a sign she was trying to keep herself in control. "Don't worry, we'll start by asking around tonight, we'll hit her regular strolls."

"I've already done that."

"I'm pretty sure you don't know how to ask questions so people will want to answer. We will get more information, don't worry." I hoped it was the truth.

Val picked up our cups and plates, her eyes focused on her chore as she spoke, "Okay, so, tonight. I'll be at your place at seven and we'll go."

"I'll see you at the gate. Don't break in again."

As we left, I made one more try to find out where she lived. "My car's just up here. Do you need a ride home?"

"Yeah, you can drop me off, but not home." Val pulled her jacket around her. "I need to take care of some things."

Well, I tried, but she clearly wants to keep some distance. Maybe later, when she trusts me more, I'd get to take her home. "Where then?"

"Okay, how about at the library? I gotta see someone there."

Rush hour was long done so I made the left turn on Georgia Street with no problem. When Val jumped out at the library, I got a glimpse of a boy waving to her from the forecourt. I hoped it was a friend not a client.

FIVE

I headed over the viaduct to Main Street toward the police station down on Main at Cordova, right on the edge of Chinatown and the Downtown Eastside.

In Chinatown, the streets were full of busy people buying groceries and making deliveries to restaurants and stores. The Downtown Eastside was not such a prosperous picture. It was all drug dealers, prostitutes and the permanently disenfranchised. But this is where I needed to be to get information on the Yeungs.

Between jaywalkers of every level of sobriety, and traffic lights every block, what should have taken ten minutes took a half hour. By the time I found parking and fed the meter, my head was pounding and I had to dry swallow a couple of aspirin. Stress didn't always come out as a headache, but when it did I had to deal with it as fast as possible to avoid a day on the couch with a towel over my eyes.

"Hi," I said to the officer behind the reception window. I'd learned it was a good idea to be pleasant to the people on reception, if you wanted to get anywhere in a bureaucracy. "I need to speak to the investigator for the Yeung murder, please."

"Do you have information?"

"I'm not sure. I need to talk to someone first."

"Name?"

"Charity Deacon."

"ID." He reached out his hand. I dug in my wallet for my driver's license and showed it to him. "Wait over there." I guess he hadn't learned that the receptionist set the tone of the organization — although given where I was, maybe he had.

I joined the other people waiting; an older woman with a hard expression, and a teenager with tattoos creeping out from the sleeves and neck of his tee shirt.

Five minutes later, a woman in uniform called my name. She introduced herself as Constable Leigh Andrews and led me upstairs to a small room with two chairs and a table.

"You have information on the Yeung case," she said, a definite statement, not question. She pulled a notebook out of her pocked and waited.

"I may have information." I knew the game we'd play. Leigh's job was to get information without sharing details. I was going to have to work hard to get what I wanted. "I witnessed an accident yesterday morning."

Leigh nodded, pen poised above her notepad. Her green eyes fixed on my face. Okay, I guess I need to give her some more.

I pushed away the memory of the last time I was in an office here. That was when I had to deliver bad news about one of their own, and it hadn't gone well. "I think I may have seen something in the crowd that you need to know about. I'm hoping you can tell me something about it."

"This would be the accident that killed Mr. Yeung."

She was cool, I'll give her that. I guess she needed to keep in control to do her job. In fact, now that I looked harder at her, I could see she'd done her best to show that control in the way she looked, too. Black curly hair pulled tightly back into a bun, uniform pressed, but a bit baggy to hide her figure.

The chair squeaked as I shifted my weight to lounge casually. "Yes. Except I think we both know it wasn't an accident."

"What makes you think that?"

"My first clue was the bullet through the guy's head. Then I notice two men watching from across the street, they seemed to be a bit too interested."

She perked up a bit at that. "Did you happen to take any pictures?"

"Yes, and video, but I want some information on the men." I had left the pictures and video at home to avoid handing them over if the cops applied pressure.

Leigh sat back. Not quite as casual as I was trying to look, but definitely pretending she didn't care. "I can't give you any information. But, tell me why you need it."

"I'm a journalist." I neglected to add, and private investigator. "I need to write a story on the connection between the two deaths."

"Which paper?"

"I'm freelance." I couldn't take the chance she would follow up if I lied about a legitimate assignment.

She hesitated. "Okay. I'll check with the liaison officer about the media information."

"Fine." I recognized an opening. "I can wait."

"The pictures and video, can I have them?"

"I have to go get them."

Leigh leaned toward me again. "Describe the men."

Now we were warming up. Note to self, don't get sucked in. "One was Indo-Canadian. He was tall maybe over six feet, well built, well dressed. The other was a shorter Asian man, also well dressed and he looked like he worked out."

She just nodded and made a note. "How long will it take you to get the pictures?"

I considered, I could probably do the round trip in less than an hour, but taking longer might be a good strategy. "A couple of hours."

"We can send you in a car, if that would be faster."

And have Delores think I was a criminal forever? "No. I'd rather not have to explain why I'm in a cop car to my neighbors."

"If the pictures are at home, you should be able to get back in less time than a couple of hours."

I should have kept my mouth shut. See, this is why I didn't bring the evidence with me. I get all caught up in everything, and forget what I'm doing. "They aren't all there."

"It might be better if we sent you in a cruiser." Her voice had suddenly become flat. I may have stepped over the line.

"It's not a problem. I just need to pull the copies together for you. I'll be back in about an hour."

"Okay." Leigh tapped her pen on the table. "I'll get the media package together while you're gone."

I wanted more than the standard media package, but that argument would have to wait until I got back.

As I stepped out of the police station, the sound of jackhammers ripped through my head. The traffic was backed up as far as I could see in both directions because of the construction. I would be sitting and idling for an hour if I drove home. I went back to my car and dropped coins in the meter to cover another two hours. The walk home would only take a half hour, and I could use the exercise.

BY THE TIME I returned with a CD of the pictures and video in my backpack, and a hotdog and coke in my stomach, the traffic jam had eased. I checked in at reception, and Leigh arrived to escort me back to a different office, this one had a computer on the desk.

She took the CD and booted up the computer. "Show me what you saw," she said passing me the mouse.

"Okay." I skipped to the scene with the two men. "See." I pointed to the screen where they stared at the mess.

"Yes, I see what you mean. Those smiles are creepy."

I was sure Leigh was going to try to avoid sharing information, but I asked anyway. "You know them, don't you? Who are they?"

Leigh handed me a slim file. "Here's the media package."

"Does it tell me who they are?"

"No." She took the mouse back and closed the video.

"I can tell they're important. Who are they?" I tried to keep my tone respectful, but the fact that she was stonewalling me told me it was something important.

"You need to stay away from these two men." She ejected the CD.

"So, who are they?" I could read the reluctance on her face. "If you don't tell me who they are, I'll have to find out some other way."

Leigh stared at the disk in her hands. It was so quiet I could hear the whir of the fan in the computer. I didn't say anything.

She finally sighed and started talking, "I don't have a lot of detail, and if I did I wouldn't be able to give it to you."

"I know you can't tell me much, but that's not going to stop me getting the information I need from somewhere."

She shut down the computer and turned to face me. Shaking her head, she said, "The tall one is Jaginder Chen, the other one is Peter Wong."

"Why should I stay away from them?"

"You can't print this. If you do, I'll deny telling you, and so will everyone else. Not just here, the RCMP won't give you anything either."

That gave me a chill. Is this what a more important case feels like? It was disturbing that Leigh was going to tell me despite department policy. "I won't print anything. My word on it."

"Jag Chen runs Xiang Investments. Peter Wong is his assistant."

"That doesn't sound like a problem." I waited, figuring she wanted to tell me more and just needed the time.

"No. We think, but can't prove, that Xiang Investments is the cover for the local arm of a Chinese gang run from mainland China, through Hong Kong."

"What makes you think they're involved?"

She stood and gestured for me to leave. "I can't tell you anything more. Stay away from them. Write another story."

SIX

That afternoon, I was in my tiny kitchen waiting for the kettle to boil, thinking about what I'd learned. The information Leigh had given me had not been earthshaking but it validated my suspicion that there was something going on. The problem was, it didn't really advance the investigation.

When the kettle boiled, I poured the water over the teabag I'd placed in my favorite red mug. Taking the tea into the office, I figured out how to start investigating Val's case.

"Okay, two things to do," I said out loud, a bad habit I needed to work on. I sat back waiting for the computer to start. "I can phone the hospitals and the morgue while I research."

I made a list of the numbers and picked up the phone. I decided to start with the hospitals, and hoped that I wouldn't need to call the morgues. I dialed St. Paul's and while the phone rang, I typed "Jag Chen" into the Google search bar.

"Hi, I'm trying to find out if an Emma Wei has been admitted in the last couple of days. She's seventeen, Asian, about five foot six, maybe a hundred and twenty pounds." I mentally crossed my fingers, hoping that the woman who had answered the phone would give me the information and not ask for some kind of authorization. And that her answer would be yes Emma was there, but not because of any major illness or injury.

She hesitated as if thinking it over, and then said, "I'll check. Hold please."

While I waited, I opened the responses to my Google. None of the links on the first three pages was pertinent. I typed 'Jaginder Chen' 'Peter Wong' in the search bar, no responses.

"Hello," the woman on the other end of the phone line said. "That was Emma Wei?"

"Yes." I felt hope rise.

"Sorry. No Emma Wei. No one answering her description either."

"Thanks."

I hung up, and then dialed Vancouver General Hospital. While I waited in the call queue, I typed "Chinese gangs Vancouver BC" in the search bar and got one hundred thirty-one thousand results.

"VGH, how can I help you?" A man with a Jamaican accent said.

The voice startled me, I'd kind of zoned out. "I'm calling about Emma Wei, was she admitted in the last few days?" I added Emma's description.

"Who are you? What relation are you to this child?"

"My name is Charity Deacon. I'm working for Emma's sister and we're worried because no one has seen her for a while."

"Hold on, now. I'll check to see who came in. It's been busy this week."

I clicked through responses on the screen while I waited, mostly blogs and editorials.

"Are you there?" The voice interrupted my search.

"Yes."

"No, there is no record of a Ms. Wei, or anyone looking like her. I hope you have better luck somewhere else."

"Thanks for checking." I hung up and dialed the next number on the list. There were dozens of hospitals in the area, but my list contained only the main ones. I'd add the others later if I needed to, but I thought it unlikely that Emma would be in a suburban hospital. I guess she could have been taken anywhere by a john, though. No reason to make the job seem bigger than it was right now.

I called the other hospitals while I followed the links on the screen. No luck, the only Asian women admitted to any hospitals in the last week were too old, or pregnant. I figured that Val would have mentioned if Emma was about to give birth.

The Google search was more productive. Four blogs mentioned two men at the head of the local Tong. All commented on the same shooting. One blog had a picture posted, Jag and Peter standing outside a storefront.

I bookmarked the blog and uncurled in a long stretch. Val would be here in an hour and there were two more numbers for me to call first. I knew that if Emma turned up dead, Val would be devastated. I didn't know all the details, but I don't think Val had anyone else to turn to. "Okay," I said aloud, "just go ahead and dial the numbers."

"Hi, I'm trying to find a young girl who has gone missing in the last week." I told the man who answered when I dialed the VGH morgue number. "Her name is Emma Wei, Asian, about five six, around hundred and twenty pounds."

"Don't sound familiar." The voice was deep and raspy. "It's possible she came in during the night shift. Can you wait while I look at their records?"

"Thanks." While I waited for him to return, I clicked through some more of the links on Google, all useless.

"She get run over?" he rasped.

"It's possible." I didn't know whether to hope it was Emma, so Val could start getting over the loss of her sister, or not.

"You want to come down and see? You gotta be a relative to get information."

I didn't relish taking Val down to identify bodies. "Before we come down, are there any tattoos?"

"Yeah. These days kids all have tats, it seems."

"Is it a butterfly?"

"I'm not really supposed to give out information. Maybe you should get the cops to call."

Crap. Part of me was glad someone took the rules seriously, but the bigger part wanted information now. "I hate to waste their time, if there's no chance it was her."

"Good point. Okay don't tell anyone where you got this." He laughed, it sounded like it was coming from his toes through a load of gravel.

"Cross my heart."

"Well, I guess if you are lying you'll end up here eventually." He laughed again. "Did you say the girl you were looking for had a butterfly?"

"Yes. Only the one tattoo."

"Then this one is still a Jane Doe with a spider on her hip."

I felt bad for the girl, but it wasn't Emma, and I was grateful for that. "Thanks."

I called the last number on the list, no Emma.

On-line I'd found information on Chinese gang business in Vancouver, prostitution, drugs, murder, and human trafficking. No surprises.

A HALF HOUR LATER, I ran down the stairs pulling on a leather jacket. I stopped at the bottom and stared at the door, or rather, at Val. "I asked you not to break in again."

"Yeah, I heard you say it." Val stood with her back to the door. This evening she was dressed in black skin-tight jeans. The waistband of the jeans sat two inches below her navel. The hem of her red tank top ended two inches above it. "I didn't like the looks I got when I was standing outside the gate."

"Fair enough." I couldn't bring myself to suggest more modest clothing, or at least more clothing. "Are you ready? I think we should start with the Downtown Eastside."

"Okay, just... I need to..."

What now? I thought she'd be the one shoving me out the door to start the search. "Look, why don't you just say it. How bad can it be?" I braced myself. Actually, what could it be that the usually brash Val stumbled on the words?

"Fine," she said with a sigh. "Look, I know you'll want more money."

"Well, why don't we wait and see." This was not a conversation I wanted to get into right now.

"No." Val held up her hand to stop me. I saw it tremble. "I don't want to wait. You know what I do, and you won't take the money I earn."

"No." I knew I'd feel soiled taking money Val made in the sex trade. "I won't take it. Val, we'll work something out don't worry. Let's get going."

I could see the tears building on her eyelashes. "What if I don't have any other way to pay you?" Val blinked the tears away as she spoke. "I know I can't do this on my own. What if I can't pay you? Will you keep looking for her?"

I preferred the brash street kid to this rapidly crumbling child. "Sit down." I handed Val a tissue and sat beside her at the table. "I won't abandon the case. But I won't take any money you earn from prostitution, or drugs."

"I sold my mother's locket to get that money yesterday." Val picked at the tissue in her lap, not looking at me. "I don't have anything else to sell."

"You don't have to pay in money."

"You want like...sex?"

"Oh, god no! Why would I want you to do that if I won't take your money?" I'd been thinking about how she'd pay me ever since I realized she wouldn't agree to me doing it for free, and I had a solution. "I meant you could help me around the house. Since you feel free to walk in without knocking, why don't you help me here when we're not trying to find Emma?"

"Won't we always be looking for her?"

"We'll have to look for her at night. I started this afternoon on the things we can do during the day."

Her eyes brightened. "Doing what?"

"Emma's not in any of the local hospitals, or the morgue."

She thought that over. "What if she didn't have ID on her?"

"There are no Jane Does matching her description."

She bit her lip then looked back at me. "What would I be doing for you?" I saw a glint of the smart mouthed survivor come back to Val's face.

"Well, my place needs cleaning and painting."

"Can't you do that yourself?"

"I hate cleaning, and I make a mess every time I try to paint. So, if you don't do it, I'll have to pay someone else."

"I can clean your place for free, but the painting will cost you."

"Are you a professional painter?" I saw that Val had fully recovered from her panic. The fear still sat below the surface, but her veneer of control was back in place. I don't ever remember being so resilient, let alone at that age.

"No, but I've painted before." She looked around as if estimating the work. "I think the painting job is worth three thousand."

I laughed. When she dropped the hardass act, she was a smart kid. "Nice try. Here's the offer. You clean my place, and paint the walls, and that will pay for the investigation." I paused, unsure that Val would accept my final condition. "And, you live here while the investigation is going on."

"Why do I have to stay here?"

"I don't want you turning tricks for food and shelter. I need to know where you are. And how to reach you, if something comes through on your sister."

I watched as Val scanned the small house, living room, small kitchen, and dining space. "Do you have two bedrooms upstairs?"

"No. We'll set you up in the den," I pointed to what I knew looked like the back of my living room. "The couch pulls out and there's a sliding door for privacy."

"I don't know." Val frowned. "How do you know I won't rip you off?"

"You haven't so far. And, you don't seem to need a key to get in."

"I'll think about it. Now, we need to start, so let's get going." Val jumped up from the chair and started for the door.

"HELLO, CHARITY." Delores Markham stood outside her front door, wearing her customary heather colored cardigan, beige knee-length skirt, and sensible brown shoes. As usual, I felt the weight of judgment she placed in just those two words. Delores was the neighborhood watch. She never actually said I was a disappointment to the community, it just dripped off her words like sap, and stuck to my conscience.

I reminded myself to be pleasant. To base my reactions on the peaceful sounds of the marina, and the bobbing masts of the boats, not the feeling that she'd caught me doing something wrong. "Hi, Delores, how are you today?"

"Fine, thank you for asking, who is your... friend?" The pause before the word friend was slight, but I noticed it.

"Name's Val." Val had her hands jammed into the pockets of her jeans. "What's it to you?"

I winced at her tone. "This is Val Wei. She'll be staying with me for a while."

"That's nice," Delores' pursed lips indicated she thought it was anything but nice. "Well, I'm glad I saw you, Charity, I need to tell you that Justin noticed your floats were sinking this morning. He asked me to give you this."

I took the business card that Delores held out. Justin, Delores' quiet, sweet husband, kept his eye on the neighborhood in a very different way from his wife. The card was for one of his, seemingly unlimited list of, people who would fix, install, or maintain what was needed in a floating house. "Thanks, I guess the otters have been poking the floats again. I'll give this guy a call."

"Yeah, look, nice to meet you and all, but we gotta get going." Val marched off to the security gate.

A HALF HOUR LATER, I was driving along Gore Street with Val staring out the window. When we left, the rain had closed down like a blanket, the buildings around the marina lurking over the streets. We made it to the Eastside in record time, despite the wet streets. It seemed like everyone else in the city had decided to stay in and be cozy.

"Pull in there." Val pointed to an open parking lot. "It's safe enough."

"Val, there's no one out. Why are we parking?" I pulled into the lot, where a couple of beaters looked abandoned in the far corner. The parking lot was full of greasy looking puddles. I was glad I'd put on some old shoes because there was no way I was going to be able to avoid getting them soaked.

"I know where we can find someone. Some crack heads don't care about the rain. If they can turn a trick, they can get a hit."

"Is that the type of person Emma hung out with?" I hoped not. The likelihood of finding Emma alive and safe dropped drastically if she was doing crack.

"No," Val snapped. "At least not when they become a crack head. They don't fucking start out that way."

"Okay." I kept my voice neutral. "Hang on a minute."

Val had become increasingly jumpy as we approached the neighborhood. She was already reaching for the seatbelt to unbuckle as I drove into the lot.

"No, let's go." Val looked at me but kept hold of the door handle.

"We can't just jump in here. Before we start, let's talk about how this is going to work. I ask the questions and you don't, right? If you have something to say, you touch my arm and wait."

"Why? What if someone's lying? They're going to lie, you know that."

"I know, and I expect it. If you start coming at them with questions it will confuse the situation. So, you'll keep a lid on it, right?" I waited for her to respond.

Val's forehead crinkled. Then she nodded before pushing the door open and stepping into the drizzle.

Following Val down the alley to the back doorway of a store, I unlocked my BlackBerry so it was ready to record any conversations. I knew from experience that people were more likely to confide in me if they didn't know I was recording. It wouldn't hold up in a court case, but I didn't take criminal cases very often so that wasn't a major issue for me.

"Sweet Marie should be out tonight, she's usually over there." Val nodded toward a doorway on the corner of the alley. It was empty. Val sighed. "I guess she's already scored."

I heard defeat creeping into her voice. "We've just started, don't worry." I looked around and saw a woman standing on the corner across Gore. "What about her."

"Juju!" Val started to cross the street, but I grabbed her hand before a car rushed past. "Whoa, slow down asshole," Val shouted after the sedan.

"Pay attention. You are no good to Emma in the hospital." I seriously wondered how she survived on the streets with, or without, a sister.

"Come on," Val said, ignoring my advice.

Juju was looking at a black sedan that slowed to a crawl in front of her. She was stick thin and dripping from standing in the rain. The driver rolled down the window, and she nodded before jumping into the back seat.

"Juju." Val called, but the woman didn't respond. "Damn!"

Defeat was turning quickly to desperation. Val looked around trying to find someone else we could talk to.

I needed to get her back in control. "Okay, calm down. We'll find someone. Just take a breath and slow down." I thought I should take her home, but I knew she wouldn't go, or wouldn't stay there.

Val stopped moving and stared at me, she was breathing rapidly and her eyes were wide. I wanted to pull her into a hug and reached out. "It's okay, we'll find her. We'll find her."

She pushed away my hand. "I'm not a kid."

We walked two blocks down Gore and then turned down another alley. We saw Juju at the end of the block, climbing out of the front seat of the black car. Val ran toward her. I unlocked the Blackberry again and pressed the voice recorder as I hurried to catch up, before Val started interrogating the woman. When I say hurried, I dodged and hopped over potholes full of water and debris.

"Hi, I'm looking for Val's sister," I called, not leaving Val an opening. "You know her, right?"

"Maybe." Juju looked at Val who was clenching her fists. "Yeah, I guess. What's she done?"

At least she was talking to us. "No one has seen her for a few days. When did you see her last?"

"A month ago. The tight-assed bitch."

Val moved closer to me.

"What do you mean?"

"She took my rocks. I worked hard for that stuff. She took them." Juju wiped her nose on the sleeve of her sweater.

Val touched my arm.

"Where did you see her?" I was surprised that Val was keeping her temper under control.

Juju gave a thin smile. "Over on the corner there, where the pervs trawl."

Val touched my arm again, pinching me. I looked at her, hoping she would see the 'wait a minute' in my glare.

I smiled back at Juju. "Did you see her get picked up?"

"No, look I gotta get paid here. I don't stand out here for my health." She looked me up and down.

I ignored the request. "What do you think might have happened?"

"Bitch got high on my rocks and..."

"Liar! You fucking liar! My sister doesn't do drugs." Val punched Juju in the stomach. Juju grabbed Val's arm and started twisting.

"Stop. Val, that's not helping." I pulled them apart. Juju slapped at Val then ran down the alley. I couldn't help but be amazed at the way she negotiated it in three inch heels. "Let's go."

Val shrugged my hand off her arm, but followed me back to the car. "Emma wouldn't have taken the crack. She wouldn't!"

"I believe you. At least I believe she wouldn't have stolen it to get high. Maybe she took it to keep Juju from killing herself."

She seemed to accept that I was on her side. "I guess I didn't think about that." She wiped her face with her arm.

"That's why you need to let me do the talking. Look there's no one else out. Let's get your stuff and settle you into my place." I was relieved that the street was empty. I needed to find a way to get Val to let me do the asking. If this is how she asked questions, it was no wonder no one had given her any information.

"Fine, drive to Glen and Cordova. You can wait there while I get my stuff."

"You don't need me to help?"

"I don't got that much stuff."

SEVEN

"What's that smell?" I walked down to the living room the next morning at 9:30. My mouth started watering as my mind started to catalog the aromas. "It smells like food."

"Do you sleep this late every day?" Val called from the kitchen. Today she was wearing a pair of jeans that didn't look painted on, and a baggy tee shirt. "I made you breakfast."

I saw she'd set the table with cutlery, napkins, and a coffee mug. I sat down as Val slid a plate of bacon eggs and pancakes in front of me. In her other hand was her breakfast.

"Was this in my kitchen?" I asked, pouring milk into the coffee. It was a rhetorical question.

Val laughed, a cross between a giggle and a hiccup. "You think a food pixie filled your fridge overnight?" She spread a thick layer of butter onto her toast. "No, I went grocery shopping. I left the bill on the counter. You can pay me back when you want."

"Thanks. I have to admit it's nice to have a real breakfast. When did you learn to cook?"

Val poured HP sauce on her eggs and dipped the toast into

the mess before she spoke, "I used to help out in my dad's restaurant before... well before we came here."

I waited but Val didn't volunteer any new information. "I guess if you're willing to cook too, we'll need to stock up on supplies."

"I don't plan to be here too long," Val said around a mouthful of bacon. "We'll find Emma and then I'm out of here."

"I hope so." When the words came out, I realized that I would already miss Val being around.

"What're we doing today?" Val wiped her mouth before taking a sip of her coffee.

I looked around at the house. It was looking messy, but not really dirty. "You could start cleaning the house. I have another case I need to work on."

She reached for my plate. I could see her hand tremble. "But we're going back tonight, right? It looks like it won't rain again, more girls will be out." Her voice had tightened.

It was really the only way to find Emma. Missing persons didn't leave a trail of breadcrumbs to follow, especially if they chose to leave. "Yes, tonight. We'll head down around seven, before dark."

I saw the fear retreat. She relaxed into a smile and looked around the room. "It won't take long to clean your place. What else should I do?"

"Most girls your age would lie on the couch and watch TV."

"Maybe you didn't notice, but I'm not most girls." Val jumped up and started to clear the table. "Can I help with your other case?"

I realized I didn't know the first thing about keeping a teenager busy. "I don't know what needs to be done yet. Start with cleaning and we'll figure out what to do about the painting."

"Your phone is vibrating," Val called from the kitchen. "Hi, Charity Deacon Investigations."

"Jeez, give me the phone," I said, smiling. I recognized the number on the display. "Lu, what's up?"

"Can you meet me?"

My way out of a debate on what Val would do with her time. "When and where?" I went back to the living room for my purse and jacket. "Okay, who's driving?" I winced when Lu said she would. "Fine, ten minutes at the foot of Broughton."

Val came out of the kitchen wiping her hands. "Where are we going?"

I had a feeling this Jag Chen thing would make Val's life seem like a Disney movie. No way was I dragging her into it. "No, we, just me. It's not about Emma. Why don't you start cleaning up? There's stuff under the sink."

Val shrugged. "Fine, when will you be back?"

"I don't know, but I don't think it will be long." I dug my wallet out and handed her four twenties. "Look, we need more groceries. Go shopping if you finish cleaning before I get back. We can figure out the painting thing tomorrow."

"You won't forget were going to find Emma tonight, right? This other case isn't more important, right?" The shake was back in her voice.

"No, it isn't. I promise I'll be back."

"Fine, should I make dinner?"

"No," I headed for the door. "You don't have to turn into my housekeeper. I'll take us out for dinner after we look for Emma. Maybe we'll be lucky and I'll be paying for three meals."

I ran up the steps from the marina, taking a deep breath of the salt air. A stray gust caught my hair and blew it over my face. I stopped, brushed my hair back, and held it with one hand while I made sure the security gate was locked. Waving at Lu, I kept to the sunlit edge of the sidewalk avoiding the fall chill that lurked in the shade of the buildings as I ran up the remaining steps.

I flopped into the seat and clicked the seatbelt shut. "So, where are we going?"

Lu had pulled away as soon as I shut the door. One day I'd learn to do the seatbelt with the door still open, but with my luck she wouldn't bother to wait for the door to shut either. Maybe I should start wearing a helmet and pads when I ride with her.

She flicked a glance at me. "I told you. I have a lead for you in the case."

"Which one?"

She laughed. "True, you have two cases. Say, are any of them paying you real money?"

I grabbed the handle as she swerved around the traffic. "Well, Val gave me two hundred, so I guess the answer is yes."

"Good. Okay, then this is about the other one." She kept her eyes on the traffic.

I swear she learned driving from sixties car chase movies.

"What's the clue?" I hung on as Lu swerved again to get around a truck. "And, how did you find it out?"

"After you sent me that email about those guys you saw, I did some checking — discretely, don't worry."

Great, just what I needed. Between Val and Lu I was going to spend half my time keeping them out of trouble. "I sent you that after I spoke to the cops. Didn't you read the email? Those guys are dangerous. If they find out you've been snooping..."

"Don't freak out. I'm being careful. I overheard this anyway, so I wasn't really snooping." Lu slammed on the brakes to avoid hitting the back of a minivan with Alberta license plates. "Anyway, you're the one living with a teenage hooker. I can't believe you moved her into your place. What does Jake think?"

"It's not up to Jake. Don't change the subject. Val's a good kid." I was surprised that I really believed that. I was coming to the conclusion that Val's street attitude was a fairly shallow shell on a highly competent young lady.

"Hang on." Lu accelerated into a left turn. "We're almost there. I'll explain in a minute." She said as she pulled into a parkade in Chinatown.

"Okay, explain." I undid the seatbelt and turned to her. "Why are we in Chinatown?"

"I said I overheard something. It was about a woman who was brought here from China by snakeheads. This old man who volunteers at HomeNow, that organization for getting housing for immigrants, was talking on the phone. He said something about a woman working in his brother-in-law's restaurant, and that she was one of the container people. He said it wasn't right, using them." Lu stopped for breath.

"And now we're on our way to talk to her? We can't just barge into the restaurant and start asking questions," I said.

Lu rolled her eyes. "I'm not done. You are so impatient. No, I asked him about her. I said I would try to help her."

Lu's definition of not snooping was a bit loose. "Okay, I hope he believed you."

"Well, I met the woman, he was telling the truth. I got her to agree to meet you and talk about those two men," Lu blurted the words out.

"I hope you didn't tell her who you were, or who I am?" I wish she'd said something first. Well, it's too late now.

"No, she thinks I'm a volunteer from United Freedom and you are, too."

I sighed. I was doing that a lot lately. "Okay, what's done is done. You have to promise me you will stay away from 'overhearing things' from now on."

She held up two fingers in the universal sign of promising. "I promise. So, are you going to talk to her?"

"Of course I'll talk to her; I can't pass this opportunity up. I just don't want you getting hurt, or worse. What's her name?"

"Winnie Mah. Come on let's go."

When we got to the foot of the stairs, we crossed the street to an alley. Typical of Chinatown, it was stacked with boxes, and vaguely organic heaps that shifted as rats pulled out their lunch. I didn't want to touch the walls, because I was sure the black coating on them was toxic. I tried to breathe shallowly to minimize the smell of rotting vegetables, car exhaust, and human waste. At the end of the alley, a door led to a restaurant kitchen.

Inside, the counters were clean and the pots on the burners were scrubbed so that the gray metal gleamed. I could see only one person in the room. She sat on a chair next to the long prep counter. Her head was hanging down, her straight black hair covering her face. Everything about her looked worn out, beige tee shirt, white—or originally white—cotton pants, and a stained cotton apron tied around her waist.

She looked like a windup toy that someone had put on a chair when it wound down.

Lu touched my shoulder and whispered. "We've got fifteen or twenty minutes. Keep it fifteen just to be on the safe side. Everyone else is out front eating before they set up for dinner."

She walked up to the woman. "Winnie, this is the person I told you about." Lu pointed to me open handed, beckoning me over. "She is trying to help stop Jag and his men from killing anyone else. You can talk to her. She's safe."

Winnie looked up, and I saw she had a black eye and a split lip. Her skin was smooth and fine textured with only a small line of tiny moles under her eyebrow. She could be any age between twenty to late thirties.

I thought that if someone tried to hit me that hard, I would have hit back, but there was no anger in her expression. Winnie looked beaten down as if she was just waiting for the next shitty thing life threw her way. I couldn't believe how brave she was being by talking to me. Even if she thought I was just an aid worker.

"Okay," she whispered. Putting her finger to her lips, Winnie stood and led us behind a row of pots. I realized we would be out of sight if someone should look into the kitchen. Not much protection, but one more step for someone to take before they saw us, might be what saves our lives.

I decided if I had only fifteen minutes we needed to get straight to the point. "Winnie, how do you know Jag Chen?"

"He's the snakehead who bring me here. Me and my sister."

I could barely hear the words, but Winnie's fear was obvious in the slight tremor in her voice. I kept pushing. Sympathy wouldn't get her free, but information would. "Where's your sister now?"

"I have not seen her since he took us from the ship. We came off the ship, and we waited in the container for long time. Many died on journey." She took a long shuddering breath and looked toward the restaurant.

When she finally talked, Winnie's words came out slowly, as if she had to think about each one. She stumbled over some of them. I couldn't tell if that was because she didn't speak English well, or if it was her split lip getting in the way.

Lu tapped me on the shoulder and pointed to her watch. I ignored her and nodded for Winnie to continue. It had only been two or three minutes. Deciding not to interrupt the flow, I didn't take notes. I'd record my impressions in the car.

"Forty women got on with me in Tianjin port. Five dead on first day, captain opened the container after two days. He throw out the bodies." She seemed to gain strength as she told the story. "On ship, we were let out of container one time every day. Six more women die because they don't eat.

Captain put their bodies in water, maybe one not dead yet."
She sobbed.

Lu shoved her arm under my nose and pointed to her watch.

"Go on," I said to Winnie as I pushed Lu's arm away. I
wasn't wasting the risk she took talking to us, just to run away
when there was still plenty of time before anyone would come
back here.

"When he take us from the container, Mr. Jag Chen keep us
in a room with cages along wall. He tell us to wash and dress in
new clothes. He tell us we have to work for him until we pay
back debt. My sister is pretty and young. Mr. Peter, Mr. Jag
Chen's man, take all the young pretty girls first. Then the rest of
women sent to work in restaurants and factories."

"What happened to you? Who did this to your face?" I tried
to keep my voice even but it was a struggle. I felt like hitting
someone.

"That man, Peter, he hit me because I get pregnant. He hit
me, and took me to a man who killed my baby." She wiped her
eyes on her apron.

"Didn't the father protect you?"

I looked over at Lu who was staring at the door to the restaurant looking ready to run.

"He was father." Winnie wiped her eyes again. "He force
me. He make me pregnant."

"I'm so sorry." I handed her a Kleenex, knowing that drying
her tears was only temporary. With the life ahead of her,
Winnie would be crying again soon. "I promise I'll do my best to
stop them."

The sound of chairs pushing away from tables and plates
being stacked, came from the restaurant. Lu grabbed my arm.
"We have to go. She'll be punished if we get caught, and I won't
be the cause of any more pain."

EIGHT

When I returned home, Val was sitting in the living room talking to Jake. I looked behind them and saw the den had been transformed into a bedroom, complete with a stack of books and an alarm clock sitting on the end table. Val finished scratching something out that she'd written on a pad, and then looked up at me.

"Good, you're back." She jumped up, holding out the paper. "I thought you might want to have a picture of Emma. I didn't have any photos, but Jake suggested I try drawing her. He says I'm pretty good."

Jake came out of the den and kissed me on the cheek. "Hey, babe. Val was here when I dropped in." He turned to go to the door. "I'll be back in a minute."

I gave him a quick hug. "Okay, she's staying here a while." I turned away and looked at the sketch.

I saw a pretty girl. She looked like Val, same dimples, and crooked front tooth. The differences were clear as well. This girl had multiple earrings hanging from one ear. Her hair was spiked on top and held in place by a large clip. Val had drawn her sister standing, wearing skin tight jeans, high heels, and a tank top. She looked tough, as though she was ready to fight. Where Val was skinny, her sister was muscled. Val's face was heart shaped, Emma's round.

"Wow, you're a good artist. Is this what she looked like the last time you saw her?" I asked. "Was she dressed like this?"

"Yes. I remember telling her to put on her jacket, it was cold. But she didn't."

"This will help. It will help a lot. Good job." I thought we would at least take it to the police. They might know her.

Val shrugged. "I should have thought of it sooner. Do you think we can go to the stores down on the Eastside today?"

"Yes. We'll do that tonight, before they close. They might not be so busy then, and maybe they'll talk."

"Can we go right after lunch?"

"Will anyone be around who knew Emma? We go now and we'll run into people who probably never saw her. Unless she hung out around her stroll during the day. Did she?"

"No. You're right" Val's shoulders dropped slightly. "I just hate sitting around waiting. Isn't there something I can do? You wanted this place painted, right? Can we go get paint?"

"I don't know what color to pick." I sighed. I hadn't counted on Val being so industrious.

She looked around. "Okay, look you should go with white, or—"

"Charity, I'm back." Jake's voice cut Val off as he walked into the room and held out a bottle of wine. "Where's lunch?"

I looked at him. "What lunch? I don't remember a lunch date."

He shrugged and threw out that sexy actor smile that made my toes curl. "Val invited me for lunch."

I turned to her. "You did? Could you have told me?"

Val held up her hands and shrugged. "Don't freak. I forgot, big deal. I had other things on my mind."

"Stop shrugging at everything." I shook my head and turned back to Jake. "Sorry, I didn't get anything in for lunch."

Val spoke before I could continue. "Wait, I didn't mean I forgot that. I just forgot to tell you. There's lunch, I made couscous and chicken."

She told Jake to sit at the table and took the bottle of wine. "It will just take a second to dish it up. Why don't you help me Charity?"

Following Val to the kitchen, I took the bottle and opened it while she arranged bowls on plates. Val tossed couscous with some shredded chicken and a mixture of peas and carrots.

"Put out the cutlery, and glasses." Val pulled three wine glasses from the cupboard. "I'll bring the food."

I smiled at the casual way she included herself in the wine drinking. Putting the third glass back, and bringing out a tumbler and a soda, I followed her back to the table.

"It looks good," Jake said taking a bowl from Val.

"Thanks." She looked at the tumbler and rolled her eyes at me before sitting next to Jake. "So, you're an actor, right?"

"Yup."

"Jake does TV shows. You must have seen him," I took a spoonful of the salad.

"No TV," she answered. "But you are good looking enough to be an actor. You know anyone famous?"

"I worked with a few Hollywood guys," he said. "I mostly work with locals."

"Oh." Val sounded disappointed. "When we find Emma, can I come watch you work?"

"I can arrange it." He nodded toward the sketch. "Does that really look like your sister?"

"Yes." Val kept her eyes on her plate and picked at the food.

"I saw her on the set last month," Jake said.

I waited for Val to react. She became still and stopped picking at her food but didn't look up.

So I asked, "Who was she with?"

"One of the money guys." I noticed Jake didn't look at Val. He refilled his glass and held the bottle up looking at me.

"Which money guy?" I asked, shaking my head about the refill.

"Eddie Monahan, you met him last month at the cast party." Jake flicked his eyes toward Val. "He's not a bad guy, just a bit sleazy. Are you sure you don't want another glass?"

There was nothing I'd like more than to sit drinking wine with Jake. "I have to work. We're going down to ask about Emma."

"Where?" Jake asked.

"Probably down on Hastings," Val answered, her voice quiet.

Jake drained his glass before saying, "Why down there?"

"That's where I saw her last," Val's voice had become uncertain, she looked at me.

"Val is my client," I said. "We can't really talk about the case. Don't worry, it's no big thing."

"No big thing?" Jake repeated. "You're going to talk to people on the Downtown Eastside about someone who was last seen there before they went missing. It's a big deal."

"No," Val said, "I know the people down there. Don't worry, we'll be fine tonight."

"Tonight?" Jake's voice was tight. He poured the last of the wine in his glass.

I didn't want to get into an argument. We were doing fine, and then he tries to take control of me. I went for the airy approach. "Jake, don't be a drama queen. It's fine. We'll be going into stores and talking to some people Val knows. We'll be out of there by nine or ten."

His eyes narrowed. "I wish you'd just stay out of places like that."

"Val, can you give us a minute?" I didn't want Jake to look like a bastard in front of the girl.

"Where am I going to go?" Val looked around. "Okay. I'll go do the dishes and you can fight in here." She picked up the empty plates and walked away, whistling.

"Who is she?" Jake asked in a low voice. "And why is she living here?"

"She's my client. Look, her sister is missing and she wanted me to help. I couldn't let her go back to the street. She's just a kid."

I could see he was putting a lot of effort into keeping his temper. He rolled his shoulders, something he did to prepare for a scene. So, he was working this discussion like an acting part. I suppressed a wave of annoyance.

He looked at the wine in his glass and said, "You're too trusting. I know you don't want to hear that, but I still don't like it."

"Can we leave it at that?" I hoped he would. "I won't take stupid chances, but I have two cases you don't like. If you can't be at peace with that, we'll be fighting all the time."

"I can't be at peace with it. I don't like the fact that you have these cases, but I could live with it. This time it's different. You've brought your case into your home. It isn't safe."

I really didn't want to have this same fight again, but my buttons were all pressed firmly in. "Safe isn't the only way to be."

"No, but it is better than dead." He put down the glass. "I think I should go."

"That's not going to solve anything. You get mad, but you won't fight. You make these dramatic statements, and want to leave." I could hear my voice rise. "I like what I do and it's sometimes dangerous. I don't tell you what parts to take. Don't tell me what jobs to take."

"Hey," Val called. "I've done the dishes. Are you still fighting?"

"We're not fighting," I called back.

"No," Jake answered at the same time.

Val came back in the room. "Look, I'm not going to do anything bad. I may be a hooker, but I'm not a thief, or a murderer. Charity is safe."

"I didn't mean..." Jake paused. "Okay, maybe I did mean you might do something to her. I'm sorry about that, but she keeps taking risks."

"Hey," I said. "I'm right here."

"Yeah, we know." Val sat down. "I'm the one who should be all pissed, because I'm the one he insulted. But, he's right. You do take risks."

"See," Jake said, "she agrees with me."

"That doesn't matter. This is about you and me. Val should be staying out of it." *Or be arguing my side.*

"No way," Val said. "I'm not on his side. You should take whatever cases you want. You just have to think about what other people might feel."

"What are you a shrink?" Jake's voice carried a chuckle. "You know, I've changed my mind. Maybe she'll be good for you."

"You're digging a hole, here." Despite my words, I felt the anger slip out of the fight. "Look, I promise I'll be careful. I always am. I haven't been hurt so far. I won't be in the future."

"I'll make sure she keeps that promise," Val said.

"Oh, yeah that makes me feel so much better." Jake shook his head. "Well, at least she can cook. Do you have coffee?"

.   .   .

I PARKED the car under a streetlight on Cordova Street, and plugged a loonie into the meter. I looked over to Val who was starting to walk toward Hastings Street. "Okay, what stores do you usually go to?"

She turned to look at me. "There are stores on Hastings that are open. We sometimes shopped there before going home."

I pulled my jacket tighter, feeling the chill of the evening. It was quiet on Cordova but I knew that as soon as we got closer to Hasting Street, the noise of the traffic, and drunks calling across the road to each other, would mix with frequent sirens.

"We can start with the stores, and then head over to Campbell Street and talk to some girls." I waited for Val to argue, or make another suggestion. When she shrugged, I started walking. "Do you know any of the people who work here?"

"Not really," Val said. "We tried not to get involved with people. Emma and me were not planning to be here much longer. And people here are kind of, you know, desperate."

"Not everyone is desperate here." I felt weird defending this area to her. The drug and desperation culture was on full display, but I could see people walking with their grocery bags through the crowds, people going home. I knew the reputation of the area, but as someone who lived in Vancouver, I also knew that the population wasn't only made up of drug dealers and sex trade workers.

She looked at me and then at the people ahead of us. "Yeah, maybe there are three people down here who are just poor and can't move away."

I don't know what had set off this particular mood, but bitter didn't suit her. "Val, I would think you'd understand how that is."

"Yeah, well you think wrong." She pulled me toward the street.

Lights from an ambulance flashed on the corner. Two attendants were talking to a woman lying on the sidewalk. I could only hear slurred words coming from her. As we turned the corner I saw large men standing around, like ticket scalpers outside GM Place. I knew their pockets weren't filled with tickets, but with little packets of powder. A few people struggled across the road, ignoring the traffic, which slowed and waited, sometimes not so patiently for them to pass. I watched as one car inched forward, herding the jaywalker.

"Where should we start?" I looked down the one block between Columbia and Carrall Streets. Two drug stores, a grocery, and a pawnbroker were open. The other businesses were locked up tight behind bars for the night.

"I guess the grocery store," Val said, her words came out grudgingly. "We used to go there. The man who's usually there is kind of okay."

"What's wrong? Should we start somewhere else?"

Val sighed. "No. This is the right place. Never mind, let's just do this."

We crossed the street at the light, and headed to the small grocery store. White metal bars protected the glass of the door and window. A bell chimed when I opened the door. I could smell cleaning fluid and spices as I stepped into the dim interior. A plate of samosas sat beside the cash. A handwritten sign read veggie $2 was taped to the edge of the plate. An old Chinese woman occupied a stool behind the register. She glared at us.

"Hi," I said, keeping a big smile on my face and holding out a copy of Emma's picture. "I wonder if you can help me. I'm looking for this girl."

The woman scowled back and shook her head.

"If you could just look at it." I stretched my smile a bit wider, and held the picture closer to the woman. "She used to come here with this girl." I pulled Val from behind me.

"Hi," Val said. "Remember me? I love your samosas. I used to buy two. Remember?"

"I don't remember," the woman said, and then looked pointedly at the plate of samosas. "You want to buy these?"

I looked at the pastries, the yellow oil pooling on the plate didn't look appetizing, but if I had to buy the plate to get information, I would. "Can you heat them up?"

"Eat them cold," the woman said, taking a plastic bag, new thank goodness, and placing all five of the samosas inside it.

She handed the bag to Val. "Okay twenty dollar."

"They are only two dollars each," I said, pushing the picture farther, almost touching the woman's nose.

"Twenty dollar." The woman glanced at the picture and held out her hand.

Val nudged me. "Give her the money."

Fishing out two tens, I handed them to the woman. "Fine, now, have you seen this girl?"

"Last week," the woman said, tucking the money into her pocket. "Not since then. Maybe Tuesday, maybe Wednesday."

"Are you sure?" I slipped the picture back into my pocket.

"Yes." The woman looked at the door. "You buying anything else? Okay, bye."

"Was she with anyone?" I asked. "Did you see where she went?"

"No." The woman picked up a Chinese newspaper and flapped it open. "You buy something, or you go."

I followed Val back out to the street. "Let's hope we have more luck at the next place."

Val shrugged, and put her hand inside the bag pulling out a samosa. "You want one of these?"

I looked at the pastry. "Maybe we should donate them to someone. We can go for dinner after we've finished here."

"I'm hungry now." Val took a bite. "I'll be hungry again, don't worry."

The cashier and pharmacist next door didn't recognize Emma.

On the way to the corner of Carrall Street, Val gave the remaining samosas to two homeless kids who were tucked into the doorway of a club.

"Things are closing down," I said. "This other drug store, and that pawnbroker look like they are the only likely places."

"I already asked at both of them, but it's probably worth checking again. What about the rooming house?" Val pointed to a dingy looking door. "She might have been in there. I didn't get to ask questions."

That seemed odd to me. I couldn't tell whether she tried but got nowhere, or for some reason she hadn't gone in. "Why didn't you get to ask questions there?"

"One of the guys who works there," she hesitated, "he is kind of a creep. I was waiting until he was gone."

"Okay. We'll go there last. Creep or not, I'll ask the questions." I nodded to the other door, "What about the mission?"

"No," Val said. "We didn't hang out there. They are for street people. We had a place to stay."

I held open the door to the drug store. Val went to the cashier. "Hey, Morris, have you seen Emma since I last saw you?"

"No, honey," the short man behind the counter said. "I kept my eye out, but like I told you, I saw her last week. She was buying condoms."

I stepped forward. "Did you see who she was with?"

He backed away as much as he could in the crowded space. "Who are you?"

Val reached over and patted his arm. "Don't worry, she's with me."

Morris looked me over and seemed to decide that Val's word was enough to validate me. "She came in here alone. I think her client was waiting outside. I saw a big guy leaning on the window, and he left when she did."

"Can you describe him?" I asked.

"No, you see the window. Can you describe anyone on the other side?"

Grime clouded the glass, and I could barely make out the shapes of people walking by. "If you think of anything else, will you call me?" I handed him my business card.

"Sure." He put the card in his pocket. "I don't think there's anything else to remember, but I'll do what I can to help."

"What about the manager, or the pharmacist?" I looked at the back of the store, where a security screen protected the pharmacist and the inventory. The top of someone's head was showing over the high counter. "Would they have seen anything?"

Val and Morris both laughed.

"They don't come out of the cage until it's time to go home," Morris said.

I noticed the top of the head shift, and a shrill voice called out, "Morris, please help the customer in the paper products."

"Yeah, they don't miss anything either." Morris lifted a section of the counter and stepped toward the back of the store.

I said goodbye to him and waited for Val on the street. "I thought you didn't know anyone."

"That's Morris, he gets to know people. But I know his name and where he works. I don't know if he has a family, or even his last name. Some people down here are kind, but close is a different thing."

We moved past a crowd of people lounging outside the rooming house as we entered. The lobby was dark, a single low-watt lamp sat on the reception desk, and one overhead fluorescent bar buzzed in front of the elevator.

I went to the desk and smiled at the guy sitting behind it. His nose, left eyebrow and lips were adorned with silver rings, which didn't match the nerd rimmed glasses he looked through. The desk was clean and contained only a registration, book and a pen chained to the desktop. Val drifted over toward the elevators.

"Hi," I said, pulling a business card from my pocket. "I'm trying to find a missing girl."

"Uh huh," the boy said, looking at the card. "Cool, private investigator. How'd you get into that gig?"

"I kind of tripped over it." I took out Emma's picture. "Have you seen this girl recently?"

"Depends what you mean by recently."

"In the last week. She was next door last week."

"She's missing?" This was not going where I wanted. While I was pretty sure he wasn't the guy Val called a creep, he didn't seem interested in answering my questions, just in asking his own.

I noticed his name tag. "Yes, Brian. That girl by the elevators is Val. The girl in the picture is her sister. Can you tell me if you've seen her, please?"

"Uh, sure." Brian rolled his eyes up. I hoped he was thinking rather than starting a fit. "Yah, she was here like, Wednesday, maybe Thursday. She signed in and took a dude up to the room."

"Do you know who the man was?" I could feel Val hovering at my shoulder.

"No." Brian made a snuffling noise that could have been a laugh. "The dudes don't put their names down."

"Can you check for Emma's signature? If we know when she was here, it will help."

Brian flipped the book open and turned a page back and forth. "Uh... yeah, here. She was here Wednesday. There's no time written down."

"Well, that helps a bit. This man, what did he look like? Do you remember?" I tried to make my voice encouraging rather than interrogating.

"Big Chinese guy. Kind of older. He had a gold tooth. Right in front, like some retro rapper."

Val leaned on the desk, but she let me keep asking the questions. "How old? Like her dad, or grandpa?"

"Maybe like an older brother. You know a way older brother, but too young to be her dad." Brian raised his eyebrows, as if asking for confirmation.

"Did they leave together?" I asked.

"It was like, the end of my shift. Let me think." He rolled his eyes up again. "He came down about five minutes before she did. I was just handing over my keys to the night shift guy, Alan, he's not here anymore, when she came down. She kinda looked like she'd been crying. Anyway, this guy was waiting for her. He was Chinese too, but younger and kinda built. Like he was working out regular."

"Did you hear his name?" I hoped we'd caught a lead.

"Naw, she just went to him and they left. Except for the crying thing, everything looked cool."

I was sure that everything wasn't cool, but at least we had one piece of information. Emma had left with someone who seemed to be cool. "If you think of anything, please call me. My number is on the card."

"Look," Brian said flipping my card back and forth in his fingers. "That guy is around sometimes. I've seen him before. I don't know who he is, but he collects girls here regular."

"Do you think he's a pimp?" I asked, feeling Val stiffen at the words.

Brian did the familiar eye roll. "Maybe, maybe not. The girls don't give him money in here, if he is. I get the vibe that he's a messenger, or something."

I reached into my pocket and took the printout of the picture of Peter and Jag. Holding it out to Brian, I asked, "Was it one of these men?"

Brian took the picture and held it close. "This is shitty resolution. You should get a better printer."

"Thanks." I reminded myself about honey and flies, and kept the sarcasm out of my voice. "Is he one of them?"

"Yeah, I think it was the short dude."

I took the picture back and pushed it into my pocket. "You've been a lot of help, thanks. You have my number. Call me if anything else comes up."

When we were on the street, Val turned to me. "Is that the guy Jake was talking about?"

"No. That was someone else." I started walking the seven blocks toward Campbell. "The guy Jake was talking about is harmless. A bit of a sleaze but harmless. This guy isn't harmless. And, even though he met her there, it doesn't mean he knows where she is."

Val hurried to follow. "We could ask him."

"He's not the kind of guy you ask these kind of questions." My mind was running through the options. There was no way I could walk up to Peter Wong and ask him questions. Maybe Leigh could bring him in and ask for us. "Let me think about the best way to deal with this, okay?"

CAMPBELL STREET WAS a depressing contrast to Hastings. Hastings was loud and full of action, Campbell was silent and empty.

We talked with the three women who were waiting for cars that never appeared. Val kept quiet while I asked the same questions of each one. No one here had seen Emma in the last few days. No one had a guess at where she was.

As we walked back to the car, I kept turning over ideas in my head. Would Emma have just taken off with a client? Where did she usually go when she needed to be alone? Was there a client who got rough?

I looked at Val as we continued to the car. She was quiet, and by the hunch of her shoulders, I assumed she was losing hope. I didn't think it was the time or place to ask Val questions unless I had to, and the answers to my questions wouldn't make an immediate difference to our case.

I knew she had to be hungry, and food was a good way to fuel ideas and hope.

"What do you want to eat?" I unlocked the car and got in while she considered.

"Whatever." It came out on a sigh.

I waited for her to buckle her seatbelt. "Chinese food?"

"Sure."

I gave up trying to drag her into the conversation. I knew there was a good place down the street. I figured we would get take-out and sit at home talking about what we should do. Then I could get some more background for the case. I missed the cheeky brat, and hoped I could draw her back out.

"Chinese it is."

I turned left on Hastings and headed back past Campbell toward the Yangtze restaurant. The light at Gore turned yellow, and this time I didn't run it.

A black SUV pulled up beside us at the light. I looked over and saw Jag Chen's profile. "Shit."

"What?" Val looked at me. "I didn't do anything."

"Not you." I calculated the odds of getting caught by them in my head. Okay, I'm not that smart. I really just asked myself if I should follow them. "We are going to take a slight detour. I need to follow these guys."

She leaned across to me and started to look up. I pushed her back into the seat. "Don't do that. These guys are bad news. We'll just follow them and see what happens."

"Okay. Well the light is green, and they'll be a block away if you don't put your foot on the gas." Val pointed at the back of the SUV.

"Smart ass." I drove through the intersection and changed lanes so that I was behind Jag's vehicle. I said a little prayer that they wouldn't pull a sudden turn.

My stomach growled.

"Let's hope they aren't going a long way," Val said, laughing. "If you don't get something to eat soon, that noise will definitely tip them off."

I reminded myself I'd wanted the smart ass back as I lifted my foot off the accelerator. A little more distance between the SUV and us was a good idea. It wouldn't do to have them see me because I tailgated. As soon as there was enough room for a small car, a minivan cut into the space. I braked and swore.

"Don't lose them." Val rolled down her window and leaned out. "They are signaling to go right."

"Get back in the car." I grabbed her shoulder and pulled her inside.

I saw the SUV turn right into the parking lot of the Yangtze. I drove past and parked on the side street. "Stay in the car," I said to Val.

"Not a chance. The one that was driving, he was the guy in the picture, right?" She opened her door with one hand and released her seatbelt with the other. "Come on, we don't want to miss them."

"Okay." I didn't have time to argue. I was too busy hoping they weren't getting take-out. "Look, don't confront them. Don't make eye contact. Stay behind me."

"Sure, sure. Let's go."

NINE

We opened the door and the warm scent of spices and hot oil wafted across us and out into the cold night. My stomach growled again.

Val giggled.

"They're in the back of the restaurant," I said, ignoring her laughter, and handing her the paper menu. "Sit here and read this."

We sat in the chairs facing the restaurant, the place where people waited for tables, or give take-out orders. I held the menu up and looked at Peter Wong and Jag Chen over the top of it. Peter seemed to be on alert. He reminded me of a Rottweiler, twitching, ready for a fight.

Jag pulled his phone out and pressed a button, said something, then pressed the button again pausing to stare at the screen before putting the phone away.

The tables nearby were filled with families and groups of friends, all talking and grabbing food from the bowls placed in the center of their tables. It occurred to me that innocent looking diners could as easily be gangsters or their families.

"You want a table?" A waiter in the traditional white shirt and black pants interrupted my surveillance.

"Take-out, please." I turned to Val and tapped the menu she was holding in front of her face. "What do you want?"

"Crispy chicken, Hot and Sour soup, Spring rolls, barbe-cued pork chow mien, Sweet and sour prawns."

"That's too much." I looked at the waiter. "The chicken, the soup, one fried rice, and the prawns." I handed him back the menu reluctantly giving up my camouflage. Following him to the cash register, I passed him my visa and signed the receipt before sitting back down.

Turning to Val, I said, "Pretend to talk to me while I watch what's going on."

"Sure, but are we just going to stare at these guys? When will we get back to finding Emma?"

"I can't think of anywhere else to look, right now. Is there somewhere she would go if she was in trouble?" So much for having this discussion over dinner. I realized I was dreading it and felt like a coward because my attention was elsewhere while it happened.

Before Val could answer, the restaurant door opened again. I saw Peter get up as the newcomer passed me. The man topped six feet, but his bulk made him look stocky. He must have weighed three hundred pounds. He was completely dressed in black, suit, shirt, and tie. Perhaps he thought it was slimming.

Peter shook the man's hand and led him back to the table.

"Holy shit," Val whispered. "That's one of Emma's clients."

I kept my eye on the table in the back. "Do you know anything about him?"

"I think he's some kind of hotshot in the neighborhood," she said.

I watched as Jag and the fat man exchanged a few words.

The fat man slid an envelope across the table to Peter, who dropped it into his coat pocket.

"Does he know who you are?" I asked as Jag and the fat man left the table and came to the door.

"No." She picked up a newspaper anyway and raised it in front of her face.

"Your order." The waiter handed me two paper bags.

Jag was almost at the door, the fat man behind him. I stood up and took the bags, almost brushing into Jag as I did. He stepped back and reached for the door. Every muscle in my body tightened as his eyes met mine. It felt like he was burning me onto his memory. His nostrils flared as though he smelled something rancid.

Val had stayed seated and reading, and I made sure my body hid her from Jag.

The whole world came to a stop.

Then the fat man smiled and gestured me through the door. On the back of his hand I saw a tattoo of a red bird, wings spread, feet extended in landing pose.

I had to move.

I muttered thanks and went through before him.

Val stayed where she was, smart girl.

Through the door, I turned right and headed for the car. The fat man stepped to the curb where a Mercedes the color of freshwater pearls waited for him.

I put the take-out bags on the back seat and waited for Val to join me. She slid into the passenger seat two minutes later.

She didn't speak the entire drive home.

"TURN ON THE OVEN," I said when we got home. "We'll grab a plateful and keep the rest warm so we can have seconds."

Val twisted the knob on the stove and pulled plates from the cupboard. I took out some serving spoons and we filled our plates.

"So, what happened after I left?" I needed to get her talking, this quiet wasn't healthy.

"Nothing." Val poked at her food.

I knew that wasn't true but it could wait. I didn't want to push her over into complete shutdown. "Okay. So, tell me about the fat man."

"I told you everything I know."

Val wouldn't look up from her plate. I had eaten half my food and she still hadn't put anything in her mouth. I could see her fingers whiten around the chopsticks. "Did she see him regularly?"

"A couple of times."

"Do you think he was the man at the rooming house? The one Brian told us about?"

She pushed her plate to the center of the table. "Maybe. Probably. Look, she had a couple of guys who would match the description. It's not like hot young guys spend a lot of money for sex."

"Okay," I said. Val was too scared, or too overwhelmed, to be helpful tonight. Making her feel useless wouldn't get me anywhere. "Look, you aren't hungry, obviously. Go to bed. I'll clean up here. We'll start fresh in the morning."

She grunted a response.

As she pulled the sliding door closed, I heard a single sob through the thin panel.

TEN

The sounds of seagulls, and a vacuum cleaner, dragged me into consciousness the next morning. I groaned myself out of bed and headed downstairs to see what Val had made for breakfast. As I did, I realized I was coming to rely on her to take care of me, and that scared me.

"Hey," I yelled over the drone of the machine. "It's clean enough."

She pulled the cord out of the wall socket and turned to me. "You have low standards."

I was glad she'd found some of her old backbone overnight. "Maybe. Is there coffee?"

"Yeah, but there's only dry toast. I didn't get butter when I shopped."

"Okay. Let's make a list, so this time we get everything. And while we're at it we should figure out what you need so you can start painting."

I ate the bread untoasted, and took the last cup of coffee from the pot.

Val plunked herself down in the chair. "What are we going to do about those guys from last night?"

Okay, maybe she was ready to talk. "Tell me what happened after I left."

"Not much." She picked at the hem of her tee shirt, unwilling to look at me.

Time for a little push. "If you don't tell me, I can't figure out what to do."

She shrugged and smoothed the tee shirt across her lap.

I shrugged too. "Fine. Then there's nothing for us to do. We didn't see anything that was criminal."

"But," she looked up at me and I could see the shine of tears in her eyes, "okay. That guy, the one that came to the door."

"Jag."

"Yeah, Jag." She sighed. "He kept looking at me and talking to the guy beside him."

"You were only sitting there for a minute." If she had come to Jag's attention, things were going to get way more complicated.

"I know, but I had nothing to be there for, you had the food. The waiter knew we were together, so he kept looking at me too."

"Did something happen?" I could feel my annoyance grow. Why wouldn't she just tell me? I couldn't show it, because it would probably just shut her down. What could have happened that made her so scared?

"I was going to get up and leave. Before I could do anything more than stand up, they came to the front of the restaurant. I think that Jag guy was going to say something, so I just ran out the door and took off."

"So, you don't know whether they were coming to talk to you or not." My gut said she had a right to be scared, but this case was full of slippery not quite right stuff. I needed something concrete to give to the cops.

She wiped her eyes. "No. But... you know."

"Yeah, I know. But we'll get them. It will be okay."

She shrugged. "What are we going to do? Emma is still missing."

"We go back out tonight and ask questions. We do some research. We keep going until we find her." I tried to sound confident, but I knew the longer it took, the less likely it was we would find her.

I also knew that the chances were when we did find her, she would be dead.

Val nodded and blew her nose. "Let's get some food in the house." She grabbed a pen and some paper.

I needed to give her some hope, and I didn't really need to give Leigh proof, just an update would do. "I can do one thing. We don't *know* anything, but I'll let the cops know what happened."

Val handed me my cell phone and started writing the grocery list.

TEN MINUTES LATER, I locked the door behind us after leaving a message on Leigh's voice mail. Val had lost the tight look around her eyes. I hoped that meant she felt we were making progress.

The grocery list was a full page of real food items, like carrots, chicken, and cucumber. We were headed for General Paint and Urban Fare. I took in a deep breath of the salty, dieselly air. The sun had a fall quality, the light was soft and yellow, but it did nothing to dispel the chill. At least there was no hint of rain, so we should be able to talk to more of the girls tonight.

"Charity, good morning," Justin's voice came from behind one of the hanging baskets. I always wondered how the Markhams ever got together. Justin was tall and thin. He dressed casually and spoke quietly, and kindly, to everyone. Delores was short and round, dressed in old lady formality and always sounded like she had judged you and found you wanting — well, maybe, that was just me.

"Hello, Justin." I pulled Val forward. "Val is staying with me for a few days." I gave her a little nudge.

"Hi. Nice flowers." She touched the brilliant petals then turned to me. "How come you don't have baskets?"

"I have brown thumbs."

Justin reached out to shake Val's hand. "Delores told me you had a visitor. I'm pleased to meet you, young lady."

"Nice to meet you too." She looked at the flowers again. "Are these impatiens?"

"Yes, they do well down here. The sea air is good for them." Justin picked a dead bloom off the side of the basket. "Did Delores mention the floats?"

"Yep, thanks. We're not listing yet, but I'll get it fixed before we do. In fact, I'll get someone to come and look at it tomorrow." I dug in my pocket for the phone number.

"Ah, Charity, there you are." Delores marched out of her front door toward us. "I'm calling a meeting of the neighbors. I think we need to discuss security."

"Has something happened?" I tried not to look at Val. If something had gone wrong, I was pretty sure Delores would be pointing fingers.

"There have been four instances of strangers wandering the finger dock in the last three days. I don't know why people can't make sure the gate is closed firmly when they come and go."

"It's a problem all right," Val said. "You expect to be safe behind a gate. But there you go, someone pulls up in boat and all their passengers just get off."

"I think a meeting is a good idea," I said. Maybe that would close the subject and we could get going. "Would you invite the boat owners too?"

"Of course." Delores wrapped her cardigan tighter. "As your friend says, they bring strangers into the street. We should have some agreement on appropriate behavior. Isn't that right, Justin?"

"Yes, dear." His voice came from behind the flowers.

"Shouldn't we be going?" Val gave my jacket a tug. "It was nice to meet you." She smiled at Delores and Justin.

"Of course, you have important things to do, I'm sure." Delores pulled the sweater around her again.

I just smiled and waved as we headed out.

"Why do you let her wind you up so much?" Val hissed at me as I slammed the gate.

How could she not see the way Delores acted? "She's always telling people what to do. And she thinks she knows everything."

"Jeez, she's just an old lady. Doesn't it bother you to have people wandering around?"

I started to laugh. "You mean teenage girls who pick the locks on security gates?"

WHEN WE GOT BACK to the house, Val unpacked the groceries, and I stacked the painting supplies in the corner. We had a plan. She would paint the place during the days when we couldn't talk to anyone about Emma. I hoped that the work would take her mind off her worry. It wasn't healthy for her to constantly fret about Emma when there was nothing we could do.

"I have to head out and help Lu with this art show," I said as I put the last roll of painter's tape on top of the drop cloth. "I'll be home early enough for us to go out again."

"What time," she called back to me. "I'll make something to eat."

"Aim for sixish." I headed upstairs to change into my only businesslike outfit.

My black dress was clean, thank God. When I added my black low heels and a silver necklace, bracelet, and earrings, I was fully ready to sell art to socialites. I heard the TV mumbling and Val whistling as I went back downstairs.

"What are you going to do while I'm gone?" I looked pointedly at the pile of painting supplies.

"I can't start that today. I won't be able to get too far and then there'll be parts where you can see where I stopped."

"Okay, so you're just going to watch TV."

"No, maybe I'll go for a walk. I'll just watch Oprah and then head out." She picked up the remote and changed the channel.

A news blurb flashed on.

"Police are investigating the brutal murder of the wife of a local community leader." A picture of the fat man from the restaurant popped onto the screen behind the newscaster. "Delia Fung was the victim of what appears to be a home invasion. The police released her identity after notifying Mr. Fung. No other details are available at this time."

"Shit," Val said. "That's the guy from yesterday."

I picked up the phone. "Yes," I said as I dialed Leigh's number. "Leigh, this is Charity. I have some information about this Fung murder. Call me."

"What are you going to tell her?" Val stared at the screen, which now showed Oprah doing her opening routine.

"I'll tell her what we know. It's not much, but we can link him to Jag Chen and that might be enough." I looked at my watch. "Damn, I have to go. I'm not sure it's safe for you to go for a walk. Stay inside until I get back."

"I don't want to be stuck in here," she said. I could hear the pout building. "I wouldn't get into trouble."

"Look." I couldn't think of a good reason other than I'd feel better knowing she was inside. "I need to help Lu, and I can't do that worrying about you. I know you think you can take care of yourself."

"I can. I have."

I grabbed my purse and jacket. "You don't know what these guys are up to. I'll be as quick as I can. Then we'll eat and go out looking for Emma. I think Leigh will call my cell, but if she calls here, tell her the facts, don't embellish."

"Fine," she said. "Don't be late."

I loved driving to Lu's house. Even in rush hour the drive through Stanley Park refreshes me. The trees border the road like a receiving line at a wedding. The Lions Gate Bridge arched toward the North Shore and the mountains that it was named after.

Today, though, I didn't get the lift from the sight. I was too worried about Val and Emma. I hated being in this stage of the investigation, the place where information didn't come together in any pattern or sense.

Lu's house was set back from the road. Trees and shrubs hid the private gardens I knew were on either side of the driveway. The guests would be stopping under the covered entrance. There would be a valet to move the cars around to the back. I drove my own car to the spaces behind the house and parked it in the far corner of the lot. I'd be one of the last to leave, so I could park out of the way.

I liked to see the full effect of her foyer when she had a show, so I walked around to the front. Lu opened the carved double doors and I saw four easels supporting canvases splashed with primary colors that seemed to glow against the cream of the walls and floor. Standing with the canvases as her backdrop, Lu was elegant in pale lilac silk and heavy gold jewelry. Today, her hair was pinned up in a pleat and her nails matched her dress.

I could never look that elegant. "This stuff is great," I said, stepping closer to the largest painting. "What do you need me to tell people about the artist?"

"She's local, and about to break out." Lu led me into the side room. "She spent five years working with the poor on the streets of Calcutta. She was inspired by the dyes they used there, the vibrancy of the colors against the desperate poverty."

I looked closer and the joy of the colors broke into a chaotic mess. I pulled back to where I could see the picture. "Well it works for her. When will people start to arrive? I have to be home by six."

"They'll be coming in about twenty minutes. We should be able to have a glass of wine and get you home in time." She handed me a stack of cards to pass out to interested patrons. "Are you meeting up with Jake later?"

"No. Val is making dinner before we go looking for her sister."

"Why do you have to get involved with this kind of stuff?" She shook her head at me. Nice hypocrisy, she's right in there with the Jag Chen stuff, but thinks I should dump Val on the cops.

"I'm an investigator." I tried to keep the annoyance out of my voice. Lu and I had this conversation almost weekly. I reminded myself she was worried because she was my friend. "I don't do missing pet cases."

"I know, but you don't usually do missing prostitute, and gang cases, either." She held up her hand to stop my response and gave my arm a squeeze. "I hope you find her. I can ask around at the society if you want. Some of the volunteers have connections on the street."

Lu worked with four charities that helped the Asian

community. And if her volunteers didn't know something, it wasn't important. I put aside my annoyance at her earlier warning and reminded myself she was just looking out for me.

I heard a car drive up. The show was about to start. My questions would have to wait until afterward.

THE SHOW WAS WINDING down and there were twenty or so sold notes on the paintings. The artist was officially discovered and the charity would receive about ten thousand dollars out of the proceeds. A success all around.

My feet were aching. Marble floors are beautiful, but try standing on them for two hours. I walked around the rooms to see what was left, there were no patrons in the house and we had five minutes before the official close. I would love to buy one of the canvases, but I wasn't in the income bracket for the prices, and I didn't have a place to hang something as large as these in my little home.

I headed to the front door to throw the lock, and a woman walked out of the first room. She must have slipped in while I checked the second one. I smiled at her and prayed she would buy fast and leave.

"Can you tell me something about the artist?" She was dressed in a designer suit. The bronze fabric of the skirt hung in sharp pleats and looked like it had been made for her. Her blond hair shone like sunshine against the darker bronze of the jacket. She touched my elbow and pointed to the painting hanging at the beginning of the display. "I like that one but I don't know why. I'm not usually attracted by such brightness."

I started with my set spiel. "She's very good at creating reactions and feelings, rather than giving you concrete features to point to that you like."

The woman smiled and touched my arm again, showing off

the huge sparkly on her ring finger. It was hard to say if she was showing off the ring, or if it was just too big to hide.

"I'd love to buy my husband a gift for his office." Her voice was low and breathy as if she was afraid to make too much noise. "He runs a successful investment company, and he's very choosy. It's so hard to find something he might like."

"If you aren't sure, you can usually lease it for a while. It's easy to arrange." I needed to hand her over to Lu. I was getting creeped out by her breathy voice and that big sparkly.

"Oh, that would be lovely." She smiled again, this time I noticed it didn't match the expression in her eyes. The look made me feel a bit like a mouse staring at the eagle about to strike.

I gestured toward the foyer. "Let me take you to Lu. She has all that information. Do you have an idea of the dimensions you'll need for his office?"

"Oh, the largest of these is fine."

She didn't move. It was like I was talking to myself.

"If you would like to wait here, I'll get Lu." I didn't want to leave her. What if the creepy vibe was because she was going to do a grab and dash with one of the pieces? But, if she wasn't going to move, it was my only choice.

"I'm sorry, I don't have time." She pulled a business card from her purse, a cream-colored plain card with her name and phone number embossed in bronze lettering. It made me wonder if she had different cards to match her outfits. "Have Mrs. Cho call me."

I took the card and showed her out. Her car was parked in front of the door, a bronze Mercedes. I watched her drive away, and glanced at her name, Mary Chen.

"OH MY GOD." I let out my breath as I spoke.

"You've been hanging around Val too much." Lu poured two glasses of Malbec and perched on one of the stools at the kitchen counter. We'd moved to the kitchen as soon as Lu had put the receipts in her safe.

"Probably," I said.

"So, you were going to ask me a question before Jase and Mrs. Sun arrived." She looked as comfortable in her dress as I would have been in jeans.

"Yeah." I remembered it was about Mr. Fung, but now I wanted to talk about Mary Chen more than anything else, particularly more than getting a lecture about Val. "Before that, do you know everyone who came to the show?"

"No." She took a sip and frowned. "That tall woman with the pink hat, I hadn't seen her before. And those two Goth girls, I don't remember ever seeing them at any of the other shows. Shelle might have invited them."

Shelle was the artist in question. She had arrived half way through the show. She'd been so shy that she'd hidden behind one of the largest canvases and turned bright red every time I introduced her to a patron.

"A woman came right at the end, very elegant in a ladies-who-lunch kind of way."

"I didn't see her. Did she want to buy something?" Lu pushed the cheese plate toward me.

"I don't know. She wanted to lease something, but when I tried to introduce her to you, she had to leave." I spread some Brie onto a rice cracker.

Lu sat forward. "Who was she? Leasing is a great source of income for the artist."

"Mary Chen." I waited trying not to hold my breath.

Lu almost choked on her wine. "As in, Mrs. Jag Chen?"

"I think so. She said her husband runs an investment firm. I had the creepiest feeling that she was there to check me out. But that couldn't be right. How could she know I was here?" Or, maybe, she was there to check out Lu.

Lu looked at me. It was the kind of look the principal gives you when you have done something, but he's not sure he can prove it. She finally asked, "Have you done anything I don't know about?"

She was so quick to accuse me. Well, maybe, she knew me well enough to know I deserved it. "That brings us back to the question I was going to ask at the beginning. I don't see how anything that I did would link this show to Jag."

"Tell me what you did. You never know, it might be coincidence." She was remarkably calm for someone who just had a gangster's wife strolling around her living room. She just picked up the little knife and carved off a piece of cheese.

I filled her in on meeting Mr. Fung, and the news of his wife's death. "I was wondering if you knew this Mr. Fung. They said he was a leader in the community."

"Oh, he's a community leader all right." Lu flung the cheese knife onto the counter. "A community of bloody thugs. He's why everyone thinks that the Chinese community is run by the fucking Tong."

I had learned not to fight with her when she went on a tirade. The best tactic was to calm her down. Despite being pretty blasé about most things, she had a very short fuse about the honor of her community. "We don't know anyone who thinks that way."

She drank the rest of her wine and refilled it, emptying the bottle. "Okay, hint taken. I'll get off the soapbox. Do you think Mr. Fung paid for his wife's death?"

"Probably." I looked at my watch. "I have to go soon. Val and I need to get down on the Eastside again."

She picked at the remnants of our snack. "When I ask

around about Emma, I'll see what I can find out about Mr. Fung." His name came out as though she'd sucked a lemon.

I had a flash of Lu getting caught by Jag. "Hey. Now who's jumping into danger?" I needed information, but not at the expense of my best friend.

"I'll be careful. I got you Winnie, didn't I? And I'm still alive and undamaged."

Now I know how she feels when I pretend there's no danger. "Yes, you are. But Mary Chen was here today. How do you know it's not because you were asking questions?"

She shook her head. "I'll be careful. If I don't help, you may not get anywhere. You know that anything that happens in Chinatown is known by the old ladies. They won't tell you anything, *gweilo*." She slapped my arm.

I knew she was right. I just didn't think it would be as safe as she thought. "Be careful. I don't want to have to come looking for you as well as Emma."

ELEVEN

I called Val as I exited the causeway, told her to put dinner on hold and meet me at the White Spot parking lot on Cardero and Georgia.

We drove to the same parking lot on Gore that we'd visited on our first night. By the time we arrived, it was twilight and the air was tinged with the odor of garbage. It could have been worse, at least the cold kept the smell down to a tolerable level. I was glad of my coat, but wished I had stopped at home and changed into warmer clothes. My art show outfit wasn't too fancy, and I could leave my jewelry hidden in the car. I wouldn't want to look like I was overdressed for the Downtown Eastside.

"Come on." Val grabbed my arm and pulled me toward the corner where two women were parading for the cars crawling past. Other women stood in doorways, or leaned against shop fronts.

"Hang on. Do you remember the rules?" I dug in my heels and made her stop. "I ask the questions."

She nodded. "Yeah, you ask the questions. I keep my mouth shut unless you say it's okay."

"If you have something to say, tap me on the arm." I waited for her to nod. "I don't want to have a repeat of the last time. No matter what someone says, you keep your temper, right?"

"Yeah, yeah. Come on I have a good feeling about tonight. We're going to find something out. I know it." She gave my arm another little tug.

I grinned. It was nice to see her being more optimistic. "Who are the women across the way?"

"The skinny one with the silver shoes is Sweet Marie." She pointed with her chin. "That's Carol in the red jacket, Elsie with the afro, and Olivia with the yellow pants. Little Boo is the one down at the end."

I didn't know why Sweet Marie earned the description of skinny. They were all under a hundred pounds. "Any reason we shouldn't start at one end of the street and work our way down?" I had a niggling feeling that she wasn't telling me everything.

"Well." She paused. "Sweet Marie should be okay, but Olivia and Emma were kinda fighting lately."

"Do you know why?" It was hard to say if Olivia would be the best place to start, or if we should just avoid her.

"Emma wouldn't say."

"Okay, then let's start with Sweet Marie." I led Val across the street.

"Hey, Val." Sweet Marie's voice rasped as though she was a four pack a day smoker. "Who's the suit?"

Hmm, not sure why I was giving off the suit vibe. "I'm helping Val look for Emma." I stepped forward, taking control.

"She still missing? Shit." Sweet Marie teetered to the corner on her four-inch platforms but the car that had stopped there turned the corner as she reached the back end. She came back to us and said, "Don't sound good, kid."

"When did you last see Emma?" I patted Val's shoulder trying to soften the implication.

"Last week, maybe Wednesday, maybe Thursday." Sweet Marie rolled her eyes. "It was busy. Welfare week."

Another person who had seen her on Wednesday, maybe Thursday. That was progress, not much, but progress. "Where did you see her?"

"Around here. Like, maybe, midnight." Sweet Marie waved at passing blue minivan. "She was with that guy. You know."

I looked at Val. "Do you know?"

She shook her head. "What guy, Marie?" I let her get away with asking because she kept her attitude out of it.

"That guy, Peter. I don't know his last name. He was hanging out with Juju, remember?"

My stomach tightened. Peter Wong? No. Val would have recognized him when we were at the restaurant.

Val frowned. "No. I never saw a guy hanging out with Juju. Well, except her pimp, but he's not Peter. What's his name? Yeah, little Tommy."

"No. This guy is new on the streets. He's built, he works out, you know." A car slowed at the curb and Marie tottered over. The window rolled down and she leaned in. "You want some company, baby?"

The door opened and Marie slid inside. "Talk to Ollie," she called before pulling the door closed.

"Shit," Val hissed. "How are we going to get Olivia to help us?"

"Did you fight with her?" I tried to think how to best approach this. I didn't think Val would just wait in the car.

"Not really." She didn't look at me. "Just... um."

"Spit it out."

"Okay. She was saying stuff about Emma. I just stood up for her."

"How did you stand up for her?" I could see Olivia heading our way.

Val shrugged, and jammed her hands in her pockets. "Maybe I called her a cheap crack whore."

"Hey, Val." Olivia sang out as she strode up to us.

"Hi," I said as I stepped between them. "I'm helping Val out. We're looking for Emma."

"Why? She owe you money?" Olivia spat into the gutter. I was beginning to understand why Val and Emma didn't like her.

"No. She's missing, and I'm worried about her." I could feel Val step behind me. "Have you seen her?"

"Yeah, maybe. Why should I help you?" She looked down at me. She must have topped out at six feet without heels, but her shoes were two-inch platform and three inch heels. I wasn't used to feeling short, and I didn't like it.

I figured it was time to cut to the chase. "Fifty bucks." I saw a gleam in her eyes and figured I might have to part with twice that.

"Seventy-five." She held out her hand.

If she didn't know how to bargain, I wasn't going to go any higher. I dug out the bills from my pocket and showed them to her. "Fifty. Tell me what you know."

She licked her lips and looked over my shoulder at Val. The smile that crossed her face started as a sneer, and got mean from there. "Down in the alley. Check there." She grabbed the bills and strolled away.

The alley she'd pointed us to was between Pender and Hastings, and I could see a blue dumpster from where we stood. Val checked the traffic and pulled me across the street when the road was clear. I didn't know what Olivia expected us to find there but I was sure it wasn't good.

"Val, hang on." I stopped as soon as my feet hit the sidewalk. "Just give me a minute. I don't think we should just go running in there."

She looked at the mouth of the alley. "But it might be a clue."

"I don't think Olivia was planning to help us." I fumbled in my pocket to grab my phone. "Let me turn on the camera."

"Hurry." Val was practically hopping with impatience. "Whatever it is, I want to know."

"Let me go first." I reached out to grab her arm, but I missed.

She dashed into the alley and came to a complete stop beside the dumpster. I moved in front of her and held my breath. Garbage had been fermenting for days. The two grocery stores had dumped rotten cabbage and something that gave off a smell that burned my eyes.

I looked around the alley and could see Val doing the same. Piles of pages from the Chinese newspaper littered the corners, a few boxes leaned in a stack against the far wall, the blue dumpster in the back and that seemed to be it. If we didn't find what Olivia wanted us to see soon, I'd have to go back and get my flashlight.

"I guess she got fifty bucks for nothing." I turned to look at Val. She was staring at the corner where the boxes were piled. I stepped closer to her and saw a pair of orange ballet style flats sticking out from behind the pile. I pulled Val away, breaking her fixed stare.

"Those are Emma's shoes." Her voice was flat, almost a whisper. "That's Emma."

"Hush." I pulled her into a hug. "Come on. We'll go out to the street. I'll call the police."

"It's Emma." She pulled away. "I can't just stand out there. We gotta get her out from under the boxes."

She moved toward the corner but I grabbed her hand. "No, let me." I didn't want her to see whatever had been done to her sister. She didn't need to have that image floating into her mind for the rest of her life

She sniffed, wiped her eyes, and then nodded before turning to face the street.

TWELVE

I pulled out my phone and dialed 911 while I walked to the boxes.

"Police," I said to the operator. "There's a dead body in the alleyway, southwest side of Gore between Pender and Hastings."

I knew they weren't going to rush for a dead body, so when I hung up I stepped closer, and tried to peer around the corner of the stack of boxes. I could see that there was a space, like someone had piled the boxes after dumping the body. I shrugged out of my jacket and used it to cover my hand, like a giant forensic mitten, while I pulled a little at the top box.

I could see a body wearing black tights and a short orange dress, but I couldn't see past the waist. I looked around and saw only Val, so no lookie loos yet.

Val was standing at the mouth of the alley, shoulders slumped and hair hanging. She shuddered as I watched. The kid was broken, not just her heart, her spirit. I knew the feeling of being alone. When Uncle Mike called about my parent's dying in India, I remember feeling empty and tiny.

I still had Mike. Val didn't have anyone.

I started to take a breath and gagged. The stench wasn't something you could get used to.

I picked up the top box and put it to the side. Then I took the next box down. Now I could see the whole body. Someone had beaten her to a mess. Her nose was flattened against her face and her mouth was sliced to her ear on the side turned up to me. Handfuls of hair were missing, and her ear was bloody where someone had ripped out the earring.

I swallowed. The brutality broke my heart, but relief brought tears to my eyes.

"Val," I heard my voice crack. "It's Juju."

Val ran toward me. I grabbed her before she got too close to Juju's body. I didn't want her to stumble into the mess.

"Let me go." She struggled in my grip but I wouldn't let her get closer.

"You can see who it is from here." I turned her so she could see Juju's face. "Don't get any closer. We don't want the cops thinking you had anything to do with this."

She stared at the bruises and split lip. "Okay. I guess you're right. Can we go somewhere else?"

I followed her to the entrance of the alley. There was nowhere to sit. "We need to be here when the cops arrive."

She looked around. "Look, why don't you wait here. I'll go get us some coffee. There's a place a few blocks away. Black, right?"

Val was shaking, and I wanted to say no. But if she was going to bolt, she could do it right now. She didn't have to pretend to go on an errand. My choice was trust her to come back, or try to keep her here.

I dug into my pocket and found a twenty-dollar bill. "Get me the biggest size they have and make sure you get sugar in yours. I don't want you passing out on me. I don't have time to sit in Emergency."

She tried to smile, but it didn't quite make it to her eyes. She jogged to the corner then turned onto Hastings.

I took some pictures of the alley and the dumpster just in case I could find some clue that the cops wouldn't notice. Then I stood on the street watching for cops – and for Val.

About five minutes after Val left, a cruiser pulled up. A tall cop climbed out of the driver's side. His partner stayed in the car. "You called us?"

"Yes. There's a body in the alley." I waited for him to identify himself but he waved to his partner, told me to wait, and then went to look in the alley.

His partner joined me on the sidewalk.

"I'm Charity Deacon, and you are?" I wasn't going to leave it to his manners this time.

"Joe Adams. That's my partner Mike Summers." He pulled a notebook from his pocket. "Why were you in the alley?"

"One of the street girls told us we could find someone we were looking for." I glanced around and there was no sign of any of the women.

"Who's we?"

"My client." I didn't like to over-share with the police.

"Where is your client?"

"Getting coffee."

Officer Summers came back to the sidewalk with his phone to his ear. "Yeah. Get someone here now." He clicked his phone shut and joined us. "It's one of the hookers. Someone beat her up badly but it looks like she shot up before so it might be an OD."

Val handed me my coffee. "Her name was Juju."

"And who are you?"

"Val Wei," she said before taking a long gulp of her frozen drink.

The two officers looked Val over. I could see them making a judgment about her reliability as they took in her clothes.

"She's my client." I stepped between her and the cops. "Can we give our statements and go?"

"I think we need to do that in the station," Summers said, obviously taking the role of bad cop.

"No way." Val took a step backward. I reached and caught the hem of her jacket.

"It's fairly simple." I kept my voice level and talked slowly. "We were looking for a missing person. We had information that she was in the alley. When we checked, we found Juju. We called the police and waited until you arrived. There, we've given our statement."

"Not so fast." Officer Adams held up his hand. "We have some questions. It will be better in the station. This street corner isn't the most private area."

"No," I said. I handed my business card to him. "You have to wait for the ambulance, and we have things to do. Contact me if you want to ask any questions later."

I turned and started to steer Val back to the car.

Officer Summers stepped in my way. "We do have questions."

I was not going to be bullied. "You have my card and I will be willing to answer any questions when you have finished with Juju's body. I am worried about my client. She's young, and this is a big shock. I want to make sure she's okay."

"I'm guessing she's not that shocked." Summers smirked. "Hookers see this kind of stuff all the time."

That was enough.

I pulled out my phone and dialed Leigh's number, saying a silent prayer she would answer.

"Detective Andrews."

"Leigh, I need you to talk to someone for me." I gave her the gist of the story. "Anyway, the officers want to take us in and question us. I was hoping you could convince them that they didn't need to do that."

"Did you have anything to do with her death?"

"No."

"Do you know anything that might help solve this crime?"

"No. I don't know anything." Suspecting Jag Chen was different from knowing.

I heard her sigh. "Okay. Let me talk to one of the officers."

I handed over the phone to Summers. After muttering two words in answer to Leigh's questions he ended the call and handed the phone back.

"We'll be in touch if we need anything. You can go." His voice was a little strained.

THIRTEEN

I parked the car, and we walked along the quay to the security gate. I could hear a few otters as they popped up and down in the water. The scent of the sea lifted my spirits a bit, but it couldn't wash the memories of the last couple of hours out of my mind.

Val straggled a few steps behind me her head hanging down, arms crossed over her chest. We went through the security gate and made it down the finger dock to my door before she sobbed out loud. I was glad she let go, she'd been holding in tears since I'd identified the body.

I opened the door and ushered her inside. She walked a few steps into the room and came to a stop.

"Val." I touched her shoulder, but she didn't react. "Hey, come on. I'll get the ice cream and potato chips. We'll veg on the couch." It seemed stupid, but I didn't know how to deal with this.

"I'll be fine. It wasn't Emma," she mumbled as she shed her jacket. "I'll just go to bed."

"It might be better to talk. It's double double chocolate ice cream."

"Fine. I'll have the ice cream. But no talking, we can watch TV."

It felt like she was humoring me, but that was okay as long as she didn't go hide in her bedroom.

"Turn on the TV. I'll get bowls." I remembered how Lu had helped start me healing when my parents died. I grabbed a bottle of wine. I'd let her have a glass. One glass wouldn't hurt.

She threw her jacket across to her bed and slumped down on the couch with the remote. I served the ice cream and a small glass of wine for her while she flipped through the channels.

She gave rapid assessments of the shows as she flipped. "Seen it. Crap. Boring. Okay."

We landed on a rerun of a Law & Order. I handed her the glass. "Here, I think you need this."

"Wow, there must be three or four sips here." She tasted the wine and nodded. "Not bad."

I took a mouthful of ice cream and felt a tiny measure of peace float through my body. The wine went well with the creaminess of the double chocolate. We watched the lawyer yell at the cops until the commercials interrupted.

"I'm okay, you know." Val didn't look at me when she spoke. "I don't need to talk. Or share or whatever."

"I know." I pretended to be absorbed by the cell phone commercial.

The program switched to news bytes. "Confidential sources close to the police have given details on the brutal murder of Mrs. Delia Fung. Stay tuned for more at eleven." I figured we knew the details on that one. Fat man hires gangster to kill wife.

"Do you want to turn to something else?" I asked. She shrugged but held onto the remote.

I took a sip of my wine and noticed her glass was empty. I poured another half glass for her and smothered the adult voice inside raging about alcohol and minors.

The program ended with the classic thunk gong. The news started with the murder of Mrs. Fung.

"We have more information on this brutal murder. The police are keeping the details from the press, but we have a source close to the investigation. The story is coming up after the commercial."

I went to the kitchen while the ads ran and served more ice cream. After a few mouthfuls, it didn't really go all that well with the wine, but I was willing to ignore the slight bitterness for the comfort of the chocolate. Val followed me in and grabbed a package of cookies. It looked like we were in for a night of gorging comfort food.

The news had returned by the time we sat back down. "We want to warn you that the information in this segment is graphic and might disturb some members of the viewing public."

The anchor turned to face a different camera and an inset picture of a house in one of the suburbs. It was chalet style, the kind with the pointy roof piece over the front door and square rooms to the side.

"This quiet Richmond neighborhood is reeling with the news that one of their neighbors met a sudden and brutal end this morning. According to our source the body was found by Mr. Fung when he returned from a meeting with local community leaders. Mrs. Fung was severely beaten. Bruises covered her entire body. The cause of death is blood loss from multiple stab wounds. Given the violence of the attack it is unclear why the neighbors did not hear screams."

"Oh, God," I said.

"It seems that post mortem, the murderer removed Mrs. Fung's right index and middle fingers."

"What?" Val pointed the remote at the television and increased the volume. "What did he just say?"

"Turn it down." I grabbed the remote and reduced the

volume to an acceptable level before turning the TV off. "What's wrong?"

She turned to me and I could see tears falling. "What did he say about the fingers?"

"The killer cut off the middle and index fingers of the right hand." I showed her by folding my fingers in as I spoke. "Why?"

She shuddered and then wiped her eyes with her sleeve. "That's what happened to our parents."

I put my hand on her arm, not sure how much comfort she'd let me give. "Tell me what happened."

She curled against me and let me put my arms around her.

"Emma and me, we came home from the mall." When she stopped, I felt her tense up.

"Just take a breath." I picked up her wine glass and handed it to her. "Take a drink."

She sat back and wiped her face again before emptying the glass.

"We lived in Kelowna. Emma and me had gone to the mall to buy a birthday present for my mom. When we got home, the front door was open. It was usually locked. Mom and dad didn't like people just walking in on them.

Emma went into the kitchen, and she told me to stop. I wish I'd listened. Mom was on the floor. There was blood everywhere. Dad was lying across the kitchen table. I..."

She stopped again, and took a deep breath that shuddered with unshed tears.

I waited.

"There was blood all over the phone. Emma had her cell out to call the police, but I stopped her. I could see mom's hand. They had cut off her right index and middle finger, I checked dad and it was the same. I could see bone." She swallowed again. "Emma said we had to go. We grabbed some small stuff and all the money we could find. Then we ran."

I made an encouraging noise and waited.

"Emma never told me what she knew. I just knew that we couldn't trust anyone. We didn't have any relatives, and nowhere to go. We got off the bus at the station on Main and Terminal, and Emma found us a place to stay. A couple of days later she came back to the room and gave me twenty bucks. She said she'd turned a trick."

She finally let the tears flow.

"I'm sorry about your mom and dad. I promise we'll find Emma." Shit, this was getting way out of my depth, but I was in too far now to drop it. I just needed to be more careful. Val crawled into bed exhausted, both emotionally and physically.

FOURTEEN

When I got up the next morning, she was still asleep and I let her stay in bed.

I needed to talk to someone who knew Jag Chen and Peter Wong. I felt like they were connected with everything in my life. Jake knew something about them from the show. Lu knew about them from the community, and now Val. Everyone I knew was tainted with their filth.

All I could think of was try to talk to Winnie again. She was my only source of information about Jag and Peter, and I hoped she would be able to point me in some direction.

I checked my watch. Assuming the staff took the same break every day, I had about an hour and a half to fill before I could hope to meet her. I looked in on Val and she was still sleeping. She seemed at peace and I didn't want to break it. I left her a note saying I would be back by one and she should wait for me. I hoped she would, but I had no idea who she'd be when she woke up, scared teenager, or tough street kid.

I filled the hour with a drive around the park. It was some-thing I did when I needed to get some perspective. The park speed limit was thirty, which left me some brain space to process problems. The scenery, forest on one side open water on the other, set the right mood for reflection. I extended the drive by leaving along Beach Avenue rather than coming around Nicola and back onto Georgia.

By the time I pulled into the same parkade as Lu had, I was feeling calm, grounded, and focused on getting information.

I took the stairs down to the street because they were closest. The smell made my eyes water, and I decided that coming back I would take the elevator.

The usual activity was happening on the street level, and although no one was paying any particular attention to me, my shoulders crawled with paranoia. I had to tell myself to relax and bring back the focus I had gained during the drive. To help quiet the crazy feeling, I looked for reflections of people following me in the shop windows, but there was nothing. While I was looking, I did see a pretty set of bowls and chopsticks. I decided to come back another time and get something to eat my take-out in next time it was Chinese food.

The back door to the restaurant was open, and I took advantage of that to peek before I went in. It looked clear so I stepped inside and saw Winnie leaning against a counter, eating something noodley from a blue china bowl.

She looked different today. No depressing beige and stained white for her this time. Her top was bright blue silk, and her black pencil-skirt fit her body perfectly. At first glance her shoes looked like genuine Jimmy Choo's, but they must have been knock-offs. There's no way she could afford them, and I couldn't believe that Jag or Peter would buy her a present that expensive.

"Winnie." I tried to keep my voice low so no one else could hear. "Can you talk?"

She looked up, her eyes going wide. She paused for a second, and then nodded and beckoned me in. She put the bowl down and pulled me behind a pot rack. The twenty huge, gray, metal soup pots hid us as effectively as if they had been a solid wall.

"They just started eating," she hissed. "I think we'll be okay for a few minutes. What do you want?"

She seemed to have grown a backbone in the last couple of days. Good for her. I felt a surge of pride that I might have been part of that change.

"I'll be quick, don't worry." I wasn't planning to waste time sneaking up on my questions. "Have you seen any other men you think are in Jag's gang?"

"Only Peter." She looked down as she said his name, her initial spunk disappearing under the weight of her situation. Maybe that spunk had really been fear. "I see other men come with Mr. Chen. I think they customers not in gang."

"I saw him the other day with a man. He was my height and older, maybe fifty or more, he was fat."

"I think I see him with men like that. Many of the customers who want girls are old, fat men." She looked out into the kitchen, and her breath caught in her throat. I noticed her eyes shine. Tears wouldn't be too far behind.

"This man had a tattoo. It looked like a parrot across the back of his hand."

"No." Winnie turned to look over her shoulder and I noticed that sound of china plates clinking as someone picked them up and piled them together. "You go." She pushed me toward the door.

Her emotions seemed to fluctuate between bossy and beaten. I shouldn't have just dropped by. If I needed to speak to her again, I'd have to work out a way to contact her. "I'm sorry. I don't mean to cause problems. I just want to help stop this."

"You go. No problems." She grabbed my elbow and steered me toward the open door. "You stay. Big problems."

God, this was difficult. If I could only talk to her for more than ten minutes at a time, I might make some headway. This way we might get a whole conversation done by the end of the year. "Look, is there any way we can talk longer?" I was almost through the door.

"No." She pushed me. "I work here, I go home. Nothing else allowed. Only now, they make me prostitute, too. Nice clothes. Bad job."

"Is there anyone else I can talk to?"

"I not know! I tell you. I come here, I go to house of man who buy my body. I go home. I not know anyone else. You go now before they see you."

I reached out and gave her arm a squeeze of reassurance. "I'll stop them, don't worry." Since when was I so sure? I guess I wasn't really. She just seemed to need some reassurance.

I headed down the short alley and almost reached the front when a black Beemer pulled in. I saw two men outlined through the tinted windows. I looked away. I didn't need to be caught staring if it was Peter and Jag.

The car pulled past me, and I turned onto the street.

As much as I knew it was dangerous, I couldn't resist the urge to look back as I turned the corner. Standing just in front of the car, staring back at me, was Jag Chen. He narrowed his eyes and snapped his fingers at Peter who was on the other side of the car.

I moved as fast as I could away from the alley and toward my car. I got there in record time, and I even ran up the stinky stairs rather than wait for the elevator. There was no one following me but the adrenaline in my system was pushing me to outrun a horde. I flopped into the driver's seat, my legs went limp, and the world went gray at the corners of my vision.

"Breathe," I whispered. "Breathe in and then breathe out." I had to break the pattern of gasps that had started when Jag's eyes met mine. If I tried to leave now, I had a good chance of crashing the car as I fainted. I sat and slowly talked myself off the stress edge. "Okay, better," I muttered as the world started to come into focus.

Now that I had myself under control, I started to worry about Winnie, and the panic started to rise again. Had I put her in danger? Oh, my God. Would Peter or Jag beat her so she would tell them what I was doing there? I couldn't go back to check to see if she was okay, that would just reinforce any suspicion they might have. All I could hope was that Winnie was a good liar.

I needed to focus on something I could change, something that would stop them completely. Something that would make Winnie safe forever.

I had promised to stop them, and I had no idea what to do. I need to know more about what they are up to. I knew they were trafficking in people, but knowing they were selling women as prostitutes and slaves didn't help me figure out how to stop them.

If I could get a look at the police file, I would be ahead of the game but that was unlikely. I also didn't want to contact Leigh since I've broken my promise to her that I would stay out of it. I should probably call her, though. I hadn't told her about Val's parents.

Shit, I'd lost the calm. I reminded myself to breathe.

I wasn't quite ready to drive yet. Driving in Chinatown was bad enough when I wasn't panicky, but now it was almost rush hour, so I had to have all my wits in place before I joined the road madness. I finally got my brain chilled out again and ready to process traffic, when the passenger door opened and I looked up into the angry face of Peter Wong.

FIFTEEN

"Who the hell are you?" he asked, grabbing my arm.

I reached across and tried to punch. Try it sometime. It's not easy to get enough leverage when you're sitting down. He grabbed my other arm and now he had me twisted in my seat, and my back was starting to spasm.

"Get out of my car." Shit. Why hadn't I locked the doors? Sitting in a car in an almost deserted parking lot wasn't a good idea at any time, let alone when you think there might be criminal psychos after you. "Who the hell are you?"

"You know who I am, bitch." He spat the words in my face. "You've been following us for a couple of days. We saw you in the Yangtze the other night." He twisted my wrist, and I gritted my teeth to keep from crying out.

"I'll scream." I managed not to whine.

"Go ahead. There's no one out there." He smiled and twisted me around more to face him. He pulled my arms apart and looked down my shirt. "I can do whatever I want for as long as I want." He licked his lips. If it weren't actually happening to me, it would be comic.

"What do you want?" I tried not to grit my teeth. I didn't

want him to know exactly how much pain he was causing, because I wanted to look tough. He probably had a good idea how much I hurt, but I didn't think he needed to be actually sure. "I don't know anything. I haven't been following you."

"Don't lie." He twisted my arms again. "I want to know why we keep seeing you. I'm not stupid, bitch. I know I keep seeing your face. If you keep denying it, you are going to understand what real pain is about." He'd loomed in closer and now he was spitting in my face with every word.

"Look." I still tried to keep my voice even, but it was time to lie like a sidewalk. "Whatever you think you've seen, I'm not following you. I was meeting someone. I was early for an appointment. I decided to come back and wait in the car."

"Bullshit."

"No, it's the truth. If I don't meet her, my friend will come looking for me."

"Who is your friend?" He smiled again and looked me over. "Maybe we can have some fun. All three of us."

"She's a cop." His eyes came back to my face immediately, and I figured there was hope of surviving. "I'm a reporter. She was giving me some information on a lotto scandal. They're investigating a store around here, because there have been too many winners in a small area like this."

"Okay." He nodded. I could almost see him calculating the odds of my lying. He probably didn't want to take the chance a cop was about to barge into his little game. On the other hand, he didn't want to give up his little game.

I saw him make his choice. It was as if a light went out in his eyes.

"If I ever see your face again, I'll come back to finish this. I'll kill you. I'll find your friends and family and kill them. Take my advice and back off." He let my arms go pushing them toward me so the tension I held in them caused me to hit my own chest; ouch.

"Back off what—" The last thing I saw was his fist coming at me.

I CAME to on my back on a gurney in a hospital hallway.

"Ms. Deacon, you're awake." I couldn't tell if she was surprised, or relieved.

"Mm, yeah." I tried to keep the talking to a minimum. It hurt my face, and my head, and my eyes. I was pretty sure that everything would continue to hurt for a while.

"Do you know where you are?"

I focused on the voice, and a nurse's Barbie pink scrubs came into focus, then a face, kind and tired. The clipboard she carried was big and metal. I couldn't help wondering how my file got that big in such a short time. I assumed, since I was in a hallway, I hadn't been here long.

"Hospital." My mouth felt like I'd been drinking glue. "Thirsty," I managed to add.

She reached over to a table tucked into an alcove across from me, and handed me a cup with a bendy straw. I forced my lips to close over the straw. It was painful, but I really needed to wet my mouth before I tried to speak again. After swallowing, I asked, "How did I get here?"

"Someone noticed your car door was open. When they saw how bad you looked, they called an ambulance." Her voice was matter of fact. I guess they're trained that way. To try to seem calm in the face of other people's pain. And I guess battered women were probably common in the ER.

She pushed a thermometer into my mouth. "The police will be by soon. They asked us to call when you came around." The thermometer beeped, she pulled it out, checked it, and wrote down the results.

I tried to think of a good reason for her not to make that call. I didn't want to answer questions, and they would be asking all kinds of them. I don't like to lie to the authorities. Okay I wasn't good at it, so I didn't like to do it.

"And your friend is on his way." She wrapped a blood pressure cuff around my arm and started pumping it up.

"Who? Ouch." Why did the pressure have to be so tight? I had enough pain in my face, I really didn't need to have any in my arm. And it didn't take my mind off the first pain, another myth destroyed. It made the throbbing stronger. I was afraid to look in case my pulse was actually making my lips swell and deflate like a cartoon.

"Sorry. I know it doesn't help to be prodded, squeezed, and poked, but we need to check you don't have any injuries other than your face before we can give you anything." She made another note on the pad. "Your friend Jake Michaels."

She flicked a light into my eye. "Nothing is broken. You have a lot of swelling where you were hit and a bump on your head on the other side. We think you hit your head on the window when you were punched. You don't have a concussion. A couple of days' rest, and you'll be fine. The bruising will fade over the next week."

"Thanks, that's good."

She looked at me, her face suddenly more pitying than tired. "It wasn't Jake, was it?"

"No." I tried to smile but my mouth wouldn't turn properly. "He would never do anything like this. When can I go?" Maybe if I got away quickly, I could avoid the police.

"Soon. The doctor wants you to stay under observation for a few hours, but you'll be able to sleep in your own bed tonight."

She hung the giant clipboard on the end on my bed. "Try to nap. The doctor will be around in about an hour."

A nap sounded like a great idea. Maybe I could nap until the pain went away. A week-long nap was just what I needed. I lay back, closed my eyes, and saw a fist coming at me. My eyes opened up in self-defense. Maybe a nap wasn't such a good idea. I lay staring up at the ceiling, counting holes in the panels.

"CHARITY, HONEY?" Jake's voice pulled me out of a nap I didn't know I had taken. I guess counting holes was as good as counting sheep. Even better, it kept the fist away.

"Who did this to you?" He reached out and pushed my hair out of my face.

I covered his hand and gave it, what I hoped was, a reassuring squeeze. "It looks worse than it is. I'll be ready to get out of here soon." The tenderness of his touch threw me off the big, strong girl pose. I could feel my throat tighten around sobs I wouldn't let out. If I cried now, I wouldn't be able to make him believe I was okay.

"Shit." Val stepped into my line of sight.

Jake hushed her. "This was because of the dead couple, wasn't it? I told you it would end in trouble. I told you to leave it alone. You should have listened to me. Are you going to stop now? Or are you going to continue until someone else is dead?"

He had that look on his face, the one that says he's locked into his own idea of what's going to happen. He was talking though tight lips, talking slowly as though he thought I might not understand.

And, he used that word I hate: should.

"No." It hurt too much to try and talk him around. And I'd never been able to do that when he got on his 'keeping Charity safe' mission. I just stated the obvious. "It's not about being safe.

It's about stopping something that is so wrong no one should let it happen." Well, obvious to me.

"That's not the right answer." Apparently, he did want to get into an argument.

"Jake, man, back off." Val pulled at his arm. "Let her be."

Jake shrugged her arm off without looking at her. "As soon as you are cleared to leave, I'm taking you home to my place, and you are going to rest. The only work you will do reading and watching TV. Even you can't get hurt doing that." He nodded as if he was agreeing for me. Screw that.

"No, I'm not! Jake, you can't tell me what to do." It sounded pretty childish, even to me. But I was hurt and trying to talk through fat lips. That made it very difficult to be articulate. "This is nothing compared to what Jag Chen and his gang are doing to those women. I'm not just crawling away and letting them get on with it."

I pushed myself up in the bed and tried to ignore the wave of bright stars that floated around the edges of my vision. We'd kept our voices low so far, but if we let ourselves get into a real fight, it wouldn't go well for Jake to be yelling at a woman who just got beaten up. I didn't want to get him in that kind of trouble. I might be mad at him right now, but I had enough sense not to get the police involved, especially since I was trying to avoid seeing cops right now.

"Where's the damn doctor? I want to get out of here. Val, can you try to find someone to discharge me? Where's my car?" I could feel my lip splitting as I hissed the words at Jake. With Val running to the nurse's station, I could let some of my anger out.

Jake straightened up. "It's in the same place you left it when you got beaten to a pulp. Apparently, the ambulance driver locked it up and put the keys in your purse."

"Fine." Damn, now I needed favor. With these stars floating

around, there was no way I could drive home let alone get back to Chinatown, and then drive home. I swallowed and tried not to sound too pitiful. "Will you drive me home?"

"Of course, did you think I would leave you here alone?" He looked hurt.

"Maybe." I lost the anger. He wasn't the bad guy here. He loved me. I didn't want to push him away because I... liked him. "I guess not."

He shook his head. "I wouldn't. Thanks for thinking so much of me. I'll go get your car and drive you home in it. If you won't stay at my place, I'll stay at yours." He held up the keys. "The doctor should have seen you by the time I get back. Don't go anywhere without me."

"Wait." I grabbed for his arm. "Take Val with you. She doesn't need to stay with me."

He walked away without saying goodbye, I heard him call Val as he passed. I know to anyone else he would be making sense, but all I heard was another way he tried to control me. I know he wasn't really, but that's how I felt. Tears prickled at the back of my eyes, and I didn't want to let them start. I wasn't sure I would be able to stop if I let the tears run. I started counting holes again to take my mind off the pain.

"MS. DEACON." A different voice penetrated my sleep. I'm going to have to get some of those holes for my bedroom ceiling.

"Yes." I tried to sound healthy enough to be discharged. The cops apparently hadn't shown up yet, so there was a slim chance of avoiding official questions.

"I'm Doctor Janssen. How are you feeling?" She held the chart in her hands, leaned in close, and checked my eyes.

"Sore and tired, but otherwise okay." I tried to keep the pain away from my voice. It wasn't easy, because I felt like I was one big throbbing pulse of pain.

"Have you been up yet?" She was looking at the metal file.

"No, but I could use the bathroom." Getting up was going to be tricky. I was feeling nauseated, and I remembered those stars from the last time I tried to get up.

"Okay. Just sit up for me, and we'll see about getting you to the bathroom." She stood back. It seemed I wasn't going to get any help. I pushed up carefully, breathing slowly to keep the stars away. I managed it without passing out, just.

Doctor Janssen nodded then said, "I'd like you to sit there for a minute while I check you over. Is that okay?"

"Sure." I needed a minute to get myself ready to stand anyway.

She took out her penlight, flicked it past my eyes, and said, "Hmm." Then she checked my blood pressure and made a note. "Hold your head still and follow my finger." She hmmed again before saying, "Go ahead and get up."

I started to follow her order, and that's when it all went sideways. My knees buckled, and I almost passed out before I could reach behind me and grab the bed. The doctor helped me lie back down.

"Okay." She nodded as if she'd expected what happened. "You don't have a concussion, but you are not all right otherwise, are you? I'll get a nurse to help you to the bathroom, and then we'll just keep you here overnight."

She left me lying on the gurney while she called over the nurse.

I hmmed back at her. I guess I just needed a good night's sleep.

SIXTEEN

It took about half an hour to get me settled in a ward with three other women already in residence. In that half hour Jake had come back to pick me up. He seemed relieved to find out I was going to have to stay in the hospital overnight. I didn't care. All I wanted to do was rest and hope the throbbing would go away while I slept.

Val patted my arm, and pulled Jake out before we could start fighting again.

I glanced around and checked out my wardmates. Across the aisle from me was an old woman. She'd introduced herself as Isobel while the orderly wheeled me the room. When I was settled, she said she had fallen a few weeks ago, and now she had a broken hip.

"Drink your milk now, young lady. You don't want to end up with fragile bones when you're my age." She'd chuckled at that and then introduced the other women who were sleeping. "That one," she said pointing to the bed to her right. "She was rock climbing and fell off. She's pretty banged up, a couple of broken ribs to go along with that arm. But her bones are strong and she'll heal. The one beside you had some operation yesterday. Don't know what it was, but she's been sleeping, or pretending to, since they wheeled her in."

I told Isabel I'd had a car accident to avoid any complicated questions. I really just wanted to fall asleep. My mind was feeling kind of dead, but the two naps left me too alert to drop off. I even counted holes, but the magic was gone.

The dinner tray came around and I picked at an overcooked macaroni and cheese casserole. I'm pretty sure they cooked it mushy for people with facial injuries. It didn't make it edible though. I was looking through a magazine that Isabel had given to me, passing it through the dinner deliveryman, when I started to get visitors.

"Charity, what the hell happened." Lu's voice interrupted my reading of an article about how to get the perfect eyebrow arch.

I sucked down the mouthful of orange Jell-O I'd been melting on my tongue, and grunted back. My jaw had swollen up to what felt like three times its size, making it difficult to do more than suck Jell-O and grunt.

My uncle Mike walked in behind Lu. He was still handsome at eighty-six. There were always women flirting with him when we went out – some of them were my age. He'd had a wild career in government security and then retired last year. I had always interpreted security as spy, but had no proof that his stories were true. "I would have thought you had more sense than to get caught. What happened?" he asked.

They pulled up chairs beside the bed and sat down. Mike leaning forward elbows on his knees, Lu perfectly straight back with her arms crossed.

"I can't talk all that well," I mumbled, hoping it would make them feel more forgiving.

"Yes. Well, take your time, we can listen slowly. Talk." Mike was bossier than Jake, but at least he wasn't trying to protect me.

"How did you know I was here?" Another mumble.

"Jake called us. He was hoping we could talk some sense into you." Lu took the Jell-O bowl from me and gave me the water bottle. "He sounded pissed. He said to tell you he would leave your car in the garage, and you call him to get you when the doctor lets you leave."

"I'd rather call a taxi." I guess I am still mad at him.

Lu sighed. "Fine. Call me if you don't want to call Jake. Now, we asked you a question." She wasn't going to be drawn away from the topic.

I looked at both of them. I knew they were concerned, and the hard ass attitude was a cover up. Well, maybe it was part of the concern. Under my gaze, Lu sat back in the chair and crossed her legs elegantly. Her hands were fidgeting in her lap, the long red nails clicking as they met. Mike just sat waiting.

"It was Peter Wong. He must have seen me coming out of the restaurant. He got in my car and punched me." Okay. It was out, and I didn't feel any better.

"Just like that. He punched you?" Lu raised an eyebrow and shook her head. "No reason, no provocation?"

"Well, no, he warned me off first." I picked at the sheets and didn't look at Lu the interrogator.

"Why would he warn you off? You must have done something to get his attention. He wasn't checking cars for possible investigators he could hit, was he?" Lu suddenly exchanged concern for suspicion. "What aren't you telling us? What have you been up to in the last couple of days?"

I waited for Mike to jump in as good cop, but he just sat there.

"Well, nothing, really." I dabbed some balm on my cracked lips. "I guess I followed them into a restaurant and maybe they saw me."

"And?" Lu could always tell when I wasn't giving the whole story.

"And, maybe, when Peter saw me today coming out of the other restaurant you took me to, he put two and two together."

"You led them to Winnie?" Lu's voice carried her shock.

Suddenly I felt sick, and it had nothing to do with my beating. "I don't think so. By the time they saw me, the staff would have returned to the kitchen. They wouldn't know who I met with, and I was in the alley, so maybe they didn't make the connection. There are lots of doors opening onto that alley." Even I heard the weakness of that.

Mike reached over and dabbed my lips with a Kleenex. He handed me the lip balm and then dabbed my cheeks. Apparently, I'd started crying.

"Who is Winnie?" he asked.

Lu looked around to see if anyone was listening, but everyone was sleeping. "One of the women smuggled in by Jag's gang."

"Who's Jag." Mike put his hand on mine. "Start at the beginning."

Lu told Mike the story as far as she knew it. I added some details about Val and her sister. Mike shook his head but I could see a smile twitching at the corner of his mouth. "You two are insane."

"That may be true." Lu stood and headed for the door. "I'll be right back. I'm going to call a friend who works nearby and find out if there were any problems at that restaurant today."

"You're in over your head, Charity." Mike's voice was resigned. He knew me too well to think I would climb out of the pool because it turned out to be deeper than I expected. I was too much like him.

"I know, but I can't step away from this." It was starting to feel like a personal mantra. "Jake and everyone I know keep telling me to back off. There's no way I can do that. Those two men are making women into slaves. They're killing people. No one seems to be able to stop them. I have to try. I'm not sure how, but Val's sister is mixed up in it. They killed her parents, they killed the Yeungs, and they killed Mrs. Fung."

I could feel my cheeks start to burn. I don't know how much was frustration and how much was anger at feeling helpless.

Mike nodded. "Yes, and you know the reason everyone who loves you keeps trying to make you stop. It isn't because we don't care about what Jag Chen is doing. It's because we don't want that to happen to you. We don't want you to go missing, or turn up dead somewhere."

"I know."

He shushed me. "I'll see what I can do about helping. I might have someone who can get you some information. At least, promise to remember to keep your options open. And always have an exit strategy."

Lu's stilettos clicked back into the room. "You are very lucky. Nothing unusual happened today. I don't know what to say to you. I know you won't back off, and I don't want you to. I want to be sure that you are careful. And you look like crap because you weren't careful. I know that doesn't excuse his behavior, but Peter Wong isn't someone you want to bait."

"Have the police been yet?" Mike seemed to want a change of subject. He dabbed at my lips again, and made me drink more water. I shook my head in answer to his question. "What do you plan to tell them?"

"As little as I can get away with. I know I have to make a report, but I don't have talk about anything other than the attack." I poked at my Jell-O and tried not to look at either of them.

"Why not tell them everything?" Lu dragged her red nails

through her hair. "It will give them something to investigate. Or have you done something illegal?"

"No. Why would you ask me that?"

"I've known you for a very long time. Why wouldn't I ask you that?" It seems Lu was still angry about Winnie. Not that I blame her, I felt like crap about it. But, Winnie was okay, so she should cut me some slack.

"I don't want them to stop me, because I don't think they can take Jag and Peter off the streets just for beating me up. I want to make sure they have enough information to do that before I hand everything over. If they can't get them put away, I think it will just get worse."

"Okay, wonder woman." Mike sighed and gave one more dab at my lips before he stood up. "You look like you need sleep. You've turned about ten shades paler since we got here. Sleep, and recover a bit, before you jump back on this tiger. I'll let you know what I find out."

"I'll come back tomorrow to get you," Lu promised. "I'll let Jake know, and he can deal with taking care of you. You should let him."

They both gave me a peck on the cheek and then left. I felt deflated. Mike was right, I was out of gas.

"It's nice your friends came to see you, dear." Isabel might be old and fragile, but she didn't miss much. I just hoped she didn't hear any details that would get me into trouble.

SEVENTEEN

I woke up. I don't know how long it was after they left. It was night, though. The light from the open blinds was the harsh artificial light of neon and halogen.

My face throbbed, and I could feel the split on my lip like a sharp piece of paper stuck there. I rolled over to get up. I couldn't do anything about my face, but I could empty my bladder. Who knows, that might even help my face.

Leigh was sitting in the chair beside my bed waiting patiently for me to notice her. Damn, I guess I wasn't going to be able to avoid the cops. I just wish it wasn't her.

"Hi." My voice was thick from sleep. "Can you wait for me to pee before we start?"

"Let me help." She smiled and put out her hand so I could pull myself up off the bed. I hadn't expected a smile, it brought up my guard.

She helped me into the small toilet beside the entrance to the ward. When I was done, she came back and helped me get into the bed. All this niceness was making my suspicion nerve itch. I wondered when bad cop was going to show up. Seriously, I always thought the good cop bad cop thing on TV was lame.

Why would someone fall for it? The thing is, her kindness made me want to cry. If she asked me to tell her anything, I'd start talking.

"You probably feel like shit. I've been there. I got beaten up last year and I can still remember how weak I was for days. I just wanted to sleep. Every time I went outside, I felt like I had to explain why I was all bruised." She grimaced. "What I remember most was the looks on the faces of people who didn't know what happened. I felt like they were judging me. Like I was responsible for being beaten up."

"I'd settle for some sympathy from strangers right now. All I've had is friends berating me." I reminded myself to stay on guard, and that she was just trying to get me to talk.

"Let's get this report done before you fall asleep again." She pulled out her notepad and pen then looked at me expectantly. "What exactly happened?"

"I was sitting in my car in a parking lot in Chinatown. Peter Wong got into my car, threatened me, and then he hit me. I don't know why."

"I'm sure you don't." Sarcasm was a bit cruel considering my sad state. "Look, I know you were a bit of a target after proving Officer Lawson was going easy on wife beaters. I'm not excusing it, but it's over. I wasn't part of it and wouldn't have been if I'd known."

"I swear I don't know anything else." I held my breath. I was so close to folding, if she put on any pressure, I would tell her everything.

"Hmm. Okay, I'll believe you, for now. For the record, please describe Peter Wong."

"He's a bit taller than me, maybe five eight. Maybe a bit taller but not over six feet. He looks like he's in his thirties, if not, he's a bit younger." I closed my eyes to help me concentrate. The fist came back at me, and I opened them again. "He has a bad scar that runs down his face, the right side, from the outside of his eyebrow to the corner of his mouth. He's lean and much stronger than he looks."

"That's a good description, thanks. We'll pull him in for questioning." She shut the book.

"No." I couldn't have him arrested. He might follow through on his threat, and then everyone would be in danger. Having his right-hand man arrested might put Jag on the defensive, and make him stop long enough for the police to move on to the next problem. Or he might just fold up shop and go somewhere else to start again.

"I can't just put this aside," Leigh argued. "The papers would be all over it if they found out we didn't follow up on violence against women. We're in enough of a bad light over the missing prostitutes as it is. I can make sure it isn't at the top of the list, though. That should buy you some time."

I couldn't believe what she'd just said. They must have given me some powerful drugs. "What do you mean, buy me some time?"

"I've given up trying to stop you. I can only stand back and let you do whatever it is you are doing." She glanced at the other beds. I'm sure she didn't want anyone overhearing our conversation any more than I did.

"Oh." I wasn't sure about believing her, but decided to give her the benefit of my drugged state. What did I have to lose? "Have you checked out my car?"

"Yes. Your boyfriend called us after he saw you. He gave us permission to search your car, but there was nothing to find except a smear of your blood on the driver's window. The blood from your lips must have sprayed on there when you hit your head." She pointed at the side of my head. It started to throb.

"He was wearing black leather gloves." I closed my eyes,

and I saw it all happen again. "He didn't touch anything, just grabbed me and hit me."

Leigh glanced around at the sleeping patients. She leaned in close and dropped her voice to a whisper. "Look, I will do what I can to help you get these guys. But I need to remind you they are dangerous, you got away pretty easy this time. This organization is mostly hidden from sight, and we never really know who's running this type of thing."

"Okay, I hear you." I knew it, here comes the lecture.

"I'm not going to tell you to be careful, that's not possible. Just be smart and aware of what's going on around you, and always know there's something going on you can't see." She looked at me as if waiting for me to say something profound.

"I said okay." I was getting tired again and it was hard to concentrate. I also had a headache to go along with all the other pain.

She switched topics abruptly. "You know something, or think you know something, we don't. It's something we couldn't have found out, right?"

"Yes, I talked to someone who can't talk to you." I wiggled my shoulders and she reached across and fixed the pillows.

"What did they say?" She sighed when I didn't answer. "Look, I can't use anything you say. If they won't talk to us, it's just hearsay and won't be of any use. If you tell me, I can try to find you some leads."

"I don't want to be the hero here." I wanted to be sure she understood it wasn't about me saving the day. It was about stopping this horrible situation. "I'm trying to get something you can use. I'm happy to give the limelight to the cops and go back to my normal life."

"I don't need to know where or how you found out. Just tell me what you know. Leave out the names of whoever you want to protect. I can't officially provide you with any help. If I did, you'd be subject to the same rules as I am. And the Mounties would just push you out of the investigation anyway." She rubbed her eyes. "I want these guys caught too. I don't care if you are looking to be a hero, I just want them stopped."

"People trafficking," I said. A yawn threatened, and I had to hold it in my throat so it wouldn't rip my lip again. "And, maybe, murder for hire. I don't know why they needed to kill the Yeungs. Maybe it was to do with the people trafficking. I think they killed Val's parents."

"The girl who reported her sister missing?"

"Yes, she's a client. What's happening with her sister?"

"They've looked in the usual places, but nothing's come up. I don't think we'll find her alive, if we find her at all. I thought the odds were crappy before you told me about the parents. That just makes it more likely we won't. Now, what do you need from me?"

No question? No lectures? This was good cop taken to the extreme.

"I don't know. I'm too tired to think. Can I call you when I get home?"

She nodded. "Look, I know I keep saying it, but this isn't meant to be a lecture. It's advice you should listen to, but it's up to you whether you do. You need to be smart around these guys. They think they are outside the law. They may get careless eventually, but until then they are likely to kill you just on the off chance you are a danger to them."

She walked out of the ward, and I lay back ready to drift off to sleep. I hoped sleep would heal me enough to get me discharged in the morning. I might even be able to suffer Jake's fussing if I had enough sleep.

EIGHTEEN

The nurse flipped through my chart and grunted before saying, "You can call someone to come and get you. The doctor signed the discharge papers."

I'd made it through the night by having short naps. The nurses had started coming in around four to check my temperature, blood pressure, and pain medication every hour. That put the end to my hopes of a long deep sleep.

I headed for the pay phone in the patient's lounge and called Lu. She needed a half hour, so I went back to the ward to wait for her, and try to make some sense of Leigh's visit.

"Are you going home today, dear?" Isabel called. "I wish I was going home. But when I get out of here I'm going to move in with my son. He's coming tonight for a visit. I'm sorry you'll miss him."

"I'm sorry I'll miss him, too." I hoped she was more comfortable than I was when it comes to having someone take care of her. "When do you think you'll be going home?"

"Oh, the doctor says another couple of weeks." She nodded her head in the direction of the sleeping woman in the bed next to me. "She hasn't had any visitors. But this one, she said her friend was coming over today."

This one, was the girl healing from the climbing accident. She limped out of the bathroom as Isabel was talking and joined the conversation.

"Yes. It's nice to have people to talk to in here." She winced as she maneuvered herself onto the bed. "When you're in here, it's like the world is going on without you. And it feels a bit like you've been forgotten if no one visits."

When I thought about these two, my short stay in the ward came into perspective. I had gotten off lucky. The world hadn't had time to pass by since I came in here. I vowed to come back and visit Isabel when I had time so she didn't feel forgotten.

I tried to smile, but my lip hurt too much. "You know, when I get home I'm going to get lectures from all my friends. They think I take too many risks. After hearing you two talk, I'm starting to look forward to it." They both laughed, and it looked like the climber regretted it from the way she grimaced.

A boy, who looked to be about ten, ran around the corner and jumped on the climber's bed.

"Hey, Julie," He yelled and then shrugged his backpack off his shoulders, pulling out a comic book. "Mom's on her way."

He was cute in the way young boys are, all perfect skin and big eyes with long lashes. His grin made me smile in return. Well, almost smile, my lip pulled and I stopped before I broke the scab on the split. He wore a private school uniform that gave him an air of studiousness. His skinned knees showed he was a much more normal boy. His mother entered the room as I watched him flip through the pages of the comic. I turned to say hello and looked right into the eyes of Mary Chen.

"Oh, do I know you?" Her brow didn't furrow, I'm not sure it could, but I saw realization dawn. "You were working at that art show. Oh, my, your face looks painful. Did you have a fight with your boyfriend?"

"No." This was too much of a coincidence for me. She hadn't come to visit Julie. I just knew she'd come to check on me. "I walked into a door."

"Maybe you should be more careful. Doors can be quite dangerous." She placed her hand on the boy's head and I saw real love replace the fake concern on her face.

"Yes." I couldn't think of anything else to say.

"Was it the door to your house?" She smiled. I'm sure Julie and Isabel thought she was been kind. All I saw was the feral light in her eyes. She looked me up and down, and I felt a shiver go through my bones.

That shiver brought out the fight in me. "No. I would have seen that coming, or I would have known it was there."

"Maybe, maybe not," she said. "We can't always see the danger right in front of us. Sometimes there are hidden traps in the places we feel the safest."

This was getting on my nerves. "I think I can take care of myself. I know what to keep my eyes peeled for."

"I'm sure." She flicked something from her skirt. "By the way, thank you for putting me in touch with that artist. My husband loves the painting. He hung it right over his desk. The colors are so striking, almost violent." She turned back to Julie and folded herself into the chair beside the bed.

I tried to keep up the innocent bystander pose for the sake of my roommates, but my nerves were jumping all over the place. I grabbed my purse and headed into the bathroom to get ready to leave. I tried to think of it as a strategic withdrawal rather than running away.

When I came back, Mary and her son were gone. It reinforced my suspicion that her visit was aimed at checking out the damage Peter had done to my spirit. Julie didn't seem concerned that the visit had been so brief.

"Your friend left quickly," I said, hoping that Julie would feel chatty.

"She had another appointment." Julie picked up a book. "She's not really a friend. I work for her, in the garden. I was kind of surprised when she said she was coming over. She doesn't seem to notice me at work. She doesn't actually seem to notice any of us outside workers."

"You're a gardener?" If I could keep her talking, maybe she would have some sliver of information for me. "I have no luck with plants. I either over water or dehydrate them."

"It's easier with outside plants. You just put in the right type of stuff and nature takes care of the rest." She chuckled, and then hugged her chest. "I'm not an expert, I just work for the gardener. It's a job that pays for my fun. I want to try a lot of variety before I settle down."

I wasn't ready to give up on her as a possible source of information. "That sounds exciting. What have you done?"

"I've been traveling for three years now. I grew up in Hamilton, Ontario and flew to Sydney, Australia on my twenty-second birthday. I waitressed in Sydney, worked as a cook on a sheep station, and led city tours in Wellington, New Zealand. I went to Europe and did some time as a nanny in Italy, pulled pints in an English pub, and picked fruit in a French orchard. I spend a couple of months in Hong Kong as a nanny to Raj – that's Mary's son." She kept her eyes on the book as she talked, almost as though she was reciting something she read there. It was weird to carry on a conversation with the top of her head.

The fact she'd worked for them before meant she was more than just a casual employee. "So, they brought you here when they moved?"

"No, I left them and worked a couple of months in Hawaii

before deciding to start the trip home. Vancouver was supposed to be a vacation, and then I was going to take the train across the country."

I was getting a bit close to the edge with my questions. I didn't want to make her feel I was interrogating her. I was mulling over my next question, 'how did you meet them again?' when Julie started talking.

"I ran into Mary at a coffee shop in West Van. She remembered me. I guess she doesn't think of the nannies as servants. Anyway, she recommended me to the gardener when I told her I was looking for some short-term work."

"Did you work as a gardener there? Hong Kong, I mean."

"No, just being nanny to Raj was a full-time job." She finally looked up. "They knew I would work hard so they gave me the job. I guess I'll need to figure out what to do next." She held up the arm in a cast. "I won't be doing any heavy work for a while. Maybe time to buy the train ticket home."

"I'm sure you'll find something. I envy you your free lifestyle. It's not something I'd be brave enough to do."

Lu walked in, and I grabbed my stuff. I was more than ready to go. I waved goodbye to my roommates and we left. I told myself to stop wondering about the coincidence of Julie being in the room with me. It didn't seem realistic that she would break her bones a few days before Peter hit me, so they could send Mary in to threaten me. It was just a coincidence and they took advantage of it.

NINETEEN

The traffic was light as we headed north on Burrard. Light or not, Lu drove in her usual crazy way back to my marina. Every traffic light turned red as we approached, and she jammed on the brakes and swore.

"Hey, I'm injured. Can you just be a bit more gentle?"

"Sorry." She patted my knee and turned left on Cordova Street.

I didn't tell her about my conversation with Julie and the threats from Mary, well what I thought were threats. I really wanted to digest the information before I had to defend my assumptions.

Lu slowed for the next light. "I'll have to just drop you off. I have to meet a new artist. Will you be okay? I can come by later and make sure you're comfortable."

"Yes, not a problem. I'll have a cup of tea. I'm sure Val will make me something I can eat." I was looking forward to some time to relax and figure out my next moves. At least Val won't tell me to stop taking chances. And, maybe, she'd have thought of a new lead for us on Emma.

Lu pulled into the circular drive and dropped me off close to the stairs. She waited until I was through the security gate before hitting the horn twice, waving, and driving off.

I took a breath and felt the comfort of my little neighborhood settle on me. My neighbors had all put out hanging baskets of fall flowers, and one of them had painted her door poppy red. My little home was looking like a plain Jane at the ball. I really needed to do some curb appeal work on my place. It was time to stop letting down the appearance of our watery street. Maybe I could get Justin to help me out. I'm sure he can find something plantlike that I can't kill.

I opened the door to my haven and realized a few hanging baskets of flowers were not going to cut it.

All my stuff was on the floor.

I could see through the living room as far as the bottom of the stairs. Every surface was covered with broken dishes and ripped apart groceries. I couldn't see anything left whole in the entire main floor. I told myself not to touch anything, but I had to step inside and look for Val. I had to know she wasn't lying dead under the mess.

Everywhere I looked was a disaster zone. The contents of my kitchen cupboard were spread over the floor. The dishes, glasses, and cutlery had been tossed everywhere. A thin layer of flour, sugar, and rice lay over everything, all Val's grocery shopping tossed into the center of the room. Pools of honey spread here and there, milk pools filled other spaces. Ketchup added a macabre tone, as though blood had spurted out of someone's veins. Broken furniture lay everywhere.

There was no sign of Val, so I stepped back to the doorway and looked at it from there so I wouldn't be tempted to start tidying up. The cordless phone was sitting in one of the milk and honey lakes. My cell phone sat on the counter, oddly undisturbed by the riot of mess everywhere. Jake must have found it in the car and brought it home for me. I was going to have to borrow a neighbor's phone, or hit the Bayshore so I didn't do any more to disturb the crime scene. There were no public phones on the streets. They just got vandalized so Telus didn't put them in.

I knocked on all the doors on the street, and no one was home. I wasn't surprised, daytime was pretty quiet around here. So, I headed to the Bayshore. The nice thing about living here was the hotel, it was always open. You could get cab, make a call, or if needed, get a room for the night.

I called Leigh directly. It didn't seem like a 911 situation.

When we finished talking, I walked back to the marina. My energy was going down fast. I sat on a bench across from my front door and tried not to fall asleep. I heard Delores and Justin talking as they walked down the finger dock. I watched them realize there was something out of the ordinary. Justin headed toward me as Delores opened their front door and took the groceries inside.

"Charity, what's wrong?" He bent his skinny frame to look me in the eye. "You look awful. Who did this to you? What can we do to help?"

"Thanks, for the offer, Justin, but I'll be fine. My face will heal. I was in St Paul's. I just got home and discovered someone broke into my place, and I'm waiting for the cops to come." His kind voice made me feel marginally better and a lot less alone and depressed. It also made me want to cry. I didn't know if it was in frustration, sadness, or both.

"Justin, what's going on?" Delores demanded. "What had happened? Why is Charity sitting on the bench? It looks like it's going to rain."

Justin passed on the news about my break-in. Delores stared at my front door as though it was somehow at fault for allowing my home to be burgled.

She tsked and looked back at me. "Come to our place while

you wait." She took my arm and exerted a bit of pressure. I stood and she pulled me along to their house. I wasn't feeling up to fighting her. The problem was her brusque attention pushed me over the edge. I sucked in a shuddering breath and started to bawl.

I couldn't stop. Justin passed me his handkerchief, and I just held it to my eyes.

"Hush." Delores put her arms around me. "It's okay. Justin will keep an eye out for the police. You and I can have a nice cup of tea while we wait. Thank goodness your young friend left just after the man finished patching your floats."

The kind word about Val started me blubbering again as I followed her into the kitchen.

I sat at her kitchen table and waited while she made the tea. Delores put fine china cups in saucers on the table, adding a plate of chocolate covered cookies. There was no chatter while she did this. It was as if she was performing a ritual: boil the water, warm the pot, add the tea, and wait while it steeped.

She sat while we waited for the tea to be ready. Her scrutiny of me didn't feel so judgmental. She reached out and patted my hand. "Charity, it will be okay. I know what I'm talking about. I don't tell many people about it, but when I was younger, before I met Justin, I lived a very different life."

I wiped my eyes, blew my nose, and made encouraging sounds. As long as she was talking, I didn't need to think about everything that had happened to me in the last few days. And the thought of Delores living a wild life was intriguing. Did she wear pants to work instead of the ladylike skirt suit?

She smiled. "I was quite an activist. I did some protesting against the Vietnam War." She poured my tea and passed me the cookie plate. "There were a lot of people who didn't think we should protest. They were very angry because their world was changing. That reaction has not changed, has it?"

She took a sip of her tea. "One night when I was going back to the motel – we were in Seattle at a big protest. Three men surrounded me on the street. They grabbed my arms and dragged me behind a dry-cleaning store." She paused and closed her eyes. When she opened them again, I saw something retreat, maybe fear. "When we were out of sight of the street, they started to beat me." She waved down my shocked reaction. "The police arrived very quickly, and I didn't receive any permanent damage. But, Charity, I'm pretty sure they would have killed me if they hadn't been interrupted."

"Oh, Delores, I'm so sorry."

"Don't be. I was doing something I thought was right." She smiled and poured more tea. "So, I know what you are feeling. You've been beaten up and your home has been ransacked. Trust me, if you are doing what you think is the right thing, it will get better. You will look back and feel like it was worth it. I promise you that is true."

"Thanks, Delores." Wow. You think you know someone and they throw something wild like that at you. "It does help. And I am doing the right thing. I know it."

She took a sip of her tea and as she put the cup down I saw the familiar Delores surface. The new, interesting Delores disappeared into hiding behind the purple heather cardigan.

"I don't want this to sound wrong, but I did see an Asian man lingering in the driveway when we went out. I didn't let him in, but you never know what the neighbors will do. It's supposed to be a secure area but, as you know, not everyone is willing to keep it that way. It doesn't seem to matter that I keep reminding them."

I didn't know what was the hardest, the feeling of helplessness that came over me, or the feeling I got that she'd just said the same thing I thought about the security around here. Was I turning into the neighborhood gossip and rule keeper? I was so used to her criticizing and judging it seemed too weird for her to act like a kindly grandmother, and a grandmother with an interesting history at that.

By the time Leigh arrived, I'd been fed tea and chocolate digestive cookies. Tea and cookies were better than painkillers. I'd gotten my tears under control. And, more importantly, Delores had fully returned to normal. She was telling me how the Smith-Joneses were causing problems by feeding otters and seagulls.

I STOOD outside my door waiting for Leigh to finish giving directions to the photographer and crime scene team. I'm not sure how much evidence they could pull out of it, but maybe flour works like fingerprint powder, who knows.

"Lucky no one was home," Leigh said.

"Well, they knew I was in the hospital." I peeked over her shoulder. Sure enough, the mess was now decorated with black smudges of fingerprint powder. "My neighbor says Val went out this morning."

She turned to me, a frown on her face. "So, when you say *they,* are you sure Val didn't do this?"

I realized I'd jumped to a conclusion about who had trashed my place. And that Leigh only knew Val as the prostitute I'd let into my house. "I don't think she would. I saw her last night. She was worried about me."

"Okay. So, you think this was Jag or Peter?"

"Or they hired someone. Don't you think so?"

Leigh shrugged. "It's not about what I think. It's about what I can prove."

I decided not to get into what I thought she could prove or not. "How long before I can get in and start cleaning?"

She looked over her shoulder at the garbage dump I used to

call a living room, and then pulled a business card from her pocket. "It looks like we'll be done in half an hour. You don't want to clean this yourself. Call this company. They specialize in cleaning crime scenes."

"Thanks, and I guess I should change the locks, too." The cookie remedy was starting to wear off. I needed to get into bed soon.

"Maybe you should just leave it alone?" Leigh made it a question.

"What, the locks?"

"No. You know I mean this thing with Jag Chen."

"I can't." I leaned against the door. "It's too late to let it be."

I saw Val coming down the gangway. She was carrying a box and I could see a French loaf sticking out of the top. I thought I'd feel relief, but I was too tired and beaten to feel anything.

"What's up?" Val shifted the box to her hip and looked Leigh up and down. "Something wrong?"

"Yeah." I nodded into the house. "We've had a visitor."

She looked into the room. "Fuck. They did this. Go arrest them." She jabbed a finger at Leigh.

"There's no proof." Leigh pushed Val's hand back. "I can't just go arrest people because someone thinks they've done something."

"No. I guess you can't. I guess only when it's some poor girl trying to get by, then you can arrest her." Val sneered.

I sighed. "Val, let it go. She's right. Let's just deal with this and get a room at the hotel tonight."

Val shook her head. "I spent the morning painting. I wanted to finish the job before you got home."

"It's okay." I needed her to stop fighting the inevitable. "You don't have to worry about it. I'll let the cleaners know. They can probably minimize the damage."

"No, it's not okay." I could hear the tears creeping into her voice. "They've got away with everything. They beat you up. They killed people. They probably have Emma. And no one is doing anything about it."

"Val." I reached for her arm. "I'm not giving up. We will get these guys. I just need to deal with this right now. We'll get them. I promise."

She looked at the mess again, then down at the box of groceries on her hip. "We need to put this somewhere until the cleaners arrive. Maybe Mrs. Markham will keep it. Then we need to get this cleaned up and the locks changed, and, yeah we need a place to sleep probably."

"Yes, ma'am." I started to smile then felt the pull of the scab. I turned to Leigh and said, "Just shut the door when you're done. I'll be back as soon as I've made arrangements."

We dropped the groceries off and headed to the hotel. If Val hadn't been there, I'm not sure if I could have made it. Her chatter kept my mind off how much I had to do. We booked a room, called the cleaner and a locksmith then grabbed a coffee at Starbucks to give me a short blast of energy.

TWENTY

The cleaners had taken an hour to arrive, and another hour to get the mess out of the house. Val and I sat on the floor of the untouched roof patio, well untouched in that they'd thrown the furniture over the side and it was out in the middle of the riptide getting ready to head for Asia. I'd called Lu, Jake, and Mike to let them know what happened, and that I had it under control. I sipped my coffee and watched boats move in and out of the marina. Val kept popping back into the house to check on the cleaners.

"The paint job is okay except for a few patches I can fix," she announced after one such trip.

"Good. How are they doing?"

"Mary, that's the tall one, said they need another twenty minutes." Val picked up the bag of chips we'd bought on our way back from the hotel. "All the crap is outside in bags. They are just finishing up on the cleaning now."

"Is there anything salvageable?" I had decided to avoid involvement in the process, but now, I was getting curious.

"Not much." She shoved a chip into her mouth and crunched it. "You are gonna need to do a major shop. I think your table is okay, but the chairs are a write-off. Your bed looks okay, but the mattress was shredded."

"We'll deal with it tomorrow." I suddenly understood Scarlett O'Hara much better. "We can probably get the big stuff ordered and then go shopping for the rest."

"When's the locksmith coming?"

I wondered why she was so interested in the schedule. "He should be here right after the cleaners are done. Are you getting bored?"

"Not really. But, I was thinking, they cut up all your clothes and mine were covered with crap from your kitchen. The cleaners threw them out."

There was no way I was going shopping when the locksmith finished. I needed to get into a bed and veg in front of a TV. "We can get clothes tomorrow."

"I could go buy us some pajamas. And maybe clothes for tomorrow. Then we could get back to finding Emma."

She had a point. We needed to get back to investigating, but I was too beat to figure out what to do next. I'd tried it while I waited for my house to be made habitable and nothing came. "I think maybe we will find Emma when I get this gang thing worked out."

She turned away and sighed. "Yeah, I was afraid of that."

"I haven't forgotten about her, Val. I just —"

"Yeah. I can put the clues together, too. They probably have her and we should go get them."

"When I go after Jag Chen, you won't be there." I waited for the explosion, but nothing happened.

"When I go shopping what should I get?"

I knew the discussion wasn't over, but I appreciated her willingness to drop it for now. Actually, I didn't relish wearing these jeans and this tee shirt tomorrow since I'd been wearing them for two days already. "We're not done talking about this,

Val. For now, you could get toothbrushes and stuff as well as pjs and clothes."

"Yeah. Just give me your visa, and I'll take care of it."

"Nice try. We'll go get some cash while the cleaners finish. Do you need a list?"

"No, just what's your size? I'll get pjs and clothes for tomorrow, and like overnight stuff."

I slurped back the last of the coffee and followed Val downstairs. After letting the cleaners know I'd be back in fifteen minutes, and that the locksmith might show up, we headed to the ATM. I gave Val money and my size and made sure she had her room key before she headed downtown.

When I got back to the house, the cleaners were writing up a receipt. The one in charge handed me my cell phone. "It's fine. We gave it a bit of a clean so you should be able to use it."

I looked around at my empty but transformed home. "The place looks great." I decided to sign a contract for regular cleaning so it would stay that way.

They took the garbage bags with them and I stood looking around the first floor of my house. It was clean, and held a table, nothing else. The first thing the cleaners had done was call a junk disposal company. My furniture had headed for the dump an hour ago.

I called my insurance agent, and he said he could be over in an hour. I really hoped he wouldn't take long, my energy would run out any time now.

My phone buzzed, the locksmith was calling from the security gate. I let him in, and he took ten minutes to change the locks.

I knew if I didn't do something while I waited, I would fall asleep on the floor, which wouldn't help me heal. I found a pen in the bottom of my purse and turned over the two receipts so I could write out a list of what we needed to buy.

I'd written, chairs, couch, TV when my phone buzzed again. I hoped it was my agent postponing until tomorrow. I could barely manage to think about what I needed, let alone something as complicated as an insurance claim.

"I see you've cleaned up the mess."

It was a man. I didn't recognize the voice but I guessed it wasn't a friend. "Who is this?" I didn't have the energy to be original.

"I'm sure you could guess if you tried."

The voice was different from Peter's but it still held menace. It was almost too polite, too controlled. I guessed it was Jag Chen. "Okay, what do you want?"

"I need to give you a message. I'm not sure you got it from my colleague." There was no real threat in his voice, but I felt threatened anyway. "You need to back off and stay backed off. Leave me and my people alone. We don't like nosy outsiders."

"I don't like gangsters. I guess no one gets everything they want, huh?" I tried to match his tone but I don't think he felt threatened.

"I'm used to getting what I want. If I don't, people get hurt. I'm sure you think you hurt now, but you have no idea." He paused. "Back off my people or your people get hurt."

"Are you kidding? How do you know I'm not recording this?" My bluffing skills aren't all that strong.

"You're not that smart, and why do you think your cell phone survived the mess? The cops haven't put a tracker on your phone. So, they won't be able to trace my call." He hung up, and I put the phone down.

I was not in the mood for games. I hurt, because he'd ordered me to be hurt. I was tired and I was going to spend a bundle of money on boring household things. I couldn't even have a cup of tea. The teabags were part of the mess the cleaners had dealt with.

I wiped my tears on my sleeve and went back to my list.

I WAS PACING out the distance I thought the new couch should cover when my doorbell buzzed. I muttered under my breath about people not keeping to the rules about security, but not too much since Val was a frequent rule breaker. I was expecting the insurance agent, so I didn't think to ask who was there. I just opened the door.

"Looks nicer than the last time I saw it." Peter Wong looked over my shoulder. He pushed me out of the way and strode into the center of my living room.

He walked around the room like a dog sniffing for places to mark his territory. I think he meant to be menacing, but his movements were a little too fast to carry off the arrogance needed for menace. I had enough experience helping Jake prepare for his roles over the years. Peter's movements made me think of the first time Jake spoke through the lines. The words were right, but there was no inflection, no passion. I looked him up and down. "What do you want?" Hey, the way I looked at it he hadn't earned politeness. Besides, I was interested. Maybe I would get an idea for a plan. Maybe he'd tell me something he shouldn't if I ticked him off.

And, maybe, just maybe, he'd leave without damaging me or my house, any more than we already were.

"You don't learn fast, do you?" He took a sudden step toward me. I stood my ground, not because I was brave but because I couldn't make my legs move. Suddenly he'd found his stride in the menacing department.

"No. I guess I'm stupid." Legs won't move, mouth won't stop, go figure.

"Yeah. You really are stupid. Most times people take the hint when we beat them up. You don't seem to have done that."

He stepped right up into my face. I could smell the barbecue sauce from the ribs he'd had for lunch. I saw shreds of the meat in his teeth.

I didn't comment. He hadn't asked a question, and, if I could control my mouth, maybe he'd fill the silence with something I wanted to know.

"Jag didn't think you understood him when he phoned." He walked a circle around me, keeping within a couple of inches of my body as he moved.

"No. He was pretty clear." I looked off into the kitchen. I felt myself doing my best to avoid eye contact, like you are supposed to do when faced with an aggressive dog.

"Maybe you didn't take him seriously." Peter stepped back a foot and then moved in toward me again. I felt my stomach tighten, and my breath sped up. It was hard to tell whether I was getting ready to fight or to flee. As the thought of running flashed into my mind, I decided I wasn't going to give him the satisfaction. Damn it, this was my home. I didn't have enough fight left in me to stand up to him, but I wasn't going to run. I stared back at him.

"Let me lay it out for you." He poked me just below my collarbone, and I stepped back to avoid falling. "Since you don't seem to be worried about yourself, we'll go after your friends. If you don't back off, then we'll hurt them. You'll have to live with the fact that you got them killed until we come for you."

"I'm calling the cops." I reached for my cell phone and he slapped it away. His face came up into mine again.

"Don't bother. You call the police, I hurt your friends." He just stared at me for a minute not saying anything.

I could see sweat sheen on his face and a tic flicking in the corner of his left eye. He stepped back and started circling again. "Your word against mine. It doesn't matter if I'm a saint or a sinner. No action from the cops without proof."

"How do you know there's no one listening to this? Maybe someone's upstairs." In my head that sounded flip and unconcerned. When I heard it aloud, it sounded petulant.

"I'll take my chances." He looked around my living room. "So, first your face, then your home, next your friends, are you too stupid to understand what I'm telling you?"

I thought about it. The magnitude of violence escalated between the attack on me and the attack on my home. He could have broken something when he hit me. I guess he could have killed me. What would it take? I didn't know any of the people threatened by these two. Okay, Winnie, but I didn't know her very well. Not like I knew my friends. I wanted to keep them from harm. I wanted to put an end to the shit these guys were bringing into my neighborhood.

I really couldn't answer his question. If not now, what would have to happen to make me stop? I'm sure there were scenarios that would make me regret not stopping, but I didn't respond to threats or ultimatums very well. So, I had to move fast enough that I never reached the regret stage.

"You don't need to do anything," I lied. "I'll back off. I don't want to get anyone hurt."

"If that's a lie there's no second chance. If you start digging, we'll know and we'll go after your friends. If you don't back off, you'll only live for three minutes after your last friend dies screaming." He'd stepped in closer while speaking and was now back in my face. "Understand?"

"Yes. Now get out of my house." I pushed him toward the door. Bravado? No. I felt like I was going to puke and needed him gone before it happened.

Peter just laughed and put his hands in his pockets as he strolled out the door, and down the walkway to the security gate. Or should I say, lack-of-security gate.

TWENTY-ONE

A night in a hotel bed, and a room service breakfast had restored my energy enough to face the prospect of going on-line to order my replacement furniture and fixings. My laptop was still in the trunk of my car because I'd intended to make some notes right after meeting Winnie. The encounter with Peter changed my schedule. If it hadn't been in my car, I'm sure Peter would have found the laptop in my place and trashed it along with everything else.

Val and I had gone shopping for food, clothes, linens, pots, plates. Pretty much anything we could shove into the car. I'd ordered a mattress yesterday, which the store delivered before we left. Val would sleep on an air mattress for a couple of nights until the couch arrived.

"Do you want some tea?" I called to Val who was pumping up her bed.

"Yeah, but I'll make it, you sit on... Oh yeah, let me get those chairs from upstairs." I'd bought a couple of cheap patio chairs to replace the ones floating away.

"Val, you don't need to take care of me. I'm not that hurt."

"I'll just get them." She ran up the stairs and I heard the sound of chair legs scraping on the patio floor.

I turned on the kettle and put teabags in two of the new mugs. Val bumped the chairs down the stairs and put them at the table. "We can sit here and talk."

"Sure." I pulled a box of cookies from the cupboard and handed them to her. "We need to figure out what to do next. I think we have to start moving faster."

She nodded. "Good. I think we need to find these guys and start following them. They'll lead us to Emma. I know it."

"No." I hadn't told Val about the phone call, or the visit, because I wasn't sure how she'd react. "We have to be more subtle. They aren't the type of people who will just let us follow them. If they have Emma, and they catch us on their tail, they'll kill her."

Val blew a small steam cloud from her mug. "I guess. So, by subtle you meant?"

"Some discrete investigation behind the scenes."

"Sounds like it will take a lot of time."

"I don't want anyone to be hurt if we can avoid it. We're not getting anywhere asking about Emma on the streets. Let me make some calls. Maybe I can find someone."

I started with Lu. Her connections in the community might help. She'd already found Winnie after all, and she'd said she would try to find out something. I left a message on her voice mail.

I called Mike next. With his connections in the security business, maybe he'd found someone who would be able to point us in a direction. I got his voice mail too. "Damn."

"What's the problem? You think people are just sitting around waiting for you to call?" Val rolled her eyes as she spoke.

"No. I just hate voice mail." I also hate not knowing if they were busy, or in Jag's hands.

I got Leigh's voice mail, too. I left a message, and then snapped the phone closed. I noticed my hands were shaking, not a good sign.

"Hey, what's wrong?" Val looked from my hands to my face.

I felt tears slide down my cheeks. I hadn't realized I was crying. Jeez, had I lost total control of myself?

"Nothing." I wiped the tears from my face.

"Bullshit!" She took the tea from me. "Tell me what's wrong. I won't stop asking until you do. I mean it."

"I don't want to talk about it." I prayed for the phone to ring, for Mike or Lu to call, or Jake. What if he had Jake?

"So, should I go get Delores?" Val asked. She sounded like she really meant it.

"No!" That's the last thing I need, wise Delores or judgmental Delores, either would be the end of me. "Okay. Yesterday, while you were shopping, I got a call from Jag. He threatened to kill my friends if I didn't stop."

"Shit. You can stop. I don't—"

"No. It just means we need to be careful. If they've decided I'm a problem, I'm never going to be free of the threat."

"But if they catch you..."

"They won't. We need to move fast. I just got a bit freaked out by three voicemails in a row. I just don't like not knowing if people are okay."

She sipped her tea again. I couldn't tell if she trusted me, or if she was just marking time until she could convince me to back off. "Maybe you should call Jake."

"He won't have anything to help us with the case."

"Duh." She rolled her eyes. "Just call him. Not everything is about getting help on the case."

She had a point, but my phone buzzed before I could dial Jake's number.

"Charity," Leigh's voice came through.

"Hi. I need some advice." I tried to think what I could ask her without triggering her 'it's too dangerous' response. "I need something I can use to speed up this job."

"You know I can't give you that," she said.

"I know, you can't tell me anything. Can you hint?"

"No. If I give you any direction, it will get in the way of the prosecution. I can't tell you what to do, or what not to do. You need to figure it out for yourself. I can tell you that we're still investigating, and so are the Horsemen."

"How do I get in touch with you when I find something?" I wasn't surprised she couldn't help, but I had to ask.

"This is my personal cell. I'll leave it on and charged." She rattled off her phone number then hung up.

"She can't help." I told Val before she started interrogating me.

VAL RETURNED from the last trip to the dumpster, talking as she walked through the door. "Hey, what about people from your other cases?"

I looked up from my notebook. "What do you mean?"

"Well, you have to talk to lots of people when you investigate, right?" She grabbed a pop from the fridge.

"Yeah, but I've called all the people who help me investigate. You were there. No one has anything useful to offer."

"I know. But maybe you have some people who don't usually help. You know, people you wouldn't normally think about asking."

I have to admit that was a great idea. My usual case was straightforward. I wasn't used to digging so deep. Before I could answer her, my phone rang. I dove for it.

"Hi, Charity," Mike said. "Listen, I'm at the airport. I have to go out of town for a while. You remember my friend, Alan Jackson?"

I did. The two of them had backpacked through Europe at the age of seventy. "Is he okay?"

"Not really." I heard the sound of a woman's voice over a PA system. "Look, I won't be able to help you with this thing. I have to get on the plane. Alan's got a bad case of the flu. You know how dangerous that can be at our age. I'm going to help take care of him. Will you look after my place?"

"Sure, no problem. Have a good flight." As much as I missed his help, I was relieved he'd be out of Jag's reach in St. Johns. I turned back to Val. "Okay, Mike's safe. Let's go through my files."

Val looked around. "What files?"

"In my office." I smiled. Up to now, I had no reason to go file diving in my office since she moved in.

"Uh, there's no office here." Val frowned like she was assessing my mental state.

"You sleep in my office."

"I figured that out, it's the only other room here, but I don't remember seeing files. If you had them they would have been trashed like the rest of your stuff."

I shuddered with the memory. "Your stuff, too, Val. I'll replace your stuff when we are done with this."

She shrugged and looked at the room where her mattress sat. "I didn't have much stuff."

"I'll still replace it." I walked into the den and knelt at the bottom of the chair rail. "My filing cabinet," I said as I hit the hidden panel. It popped open. Inside, were shelves covered in piles of documents.

"That is so cool." Val crouched beside me. "It's like a real secret compartment."

"I know. I had it built when I bought the house. This is the first time it's actually been worth it." It was a bit of a pain to have it down so low, the top shelf only came to my mid-thigh, but I liked being able to hide my work away and have a home, not an office.

"How come you didn't organize it?" Val reached for the first pile.

"I never got around to it. I guess we can do it while we look for contacts." I took the last file and placed it on top of a heap. The documents all slid out and scattered across the floor. "Damn."

"You need some office supplies to do a good job, but we can at least sort them out." She picked up the mess as she talked.

I carried the files to the table. I was looking forward to when I had my new furniture in place. "You know, people make a living as professional organizers."

"No kidding. Maybe Emma and me can start a business." She stood beside me at the table. "Man, that's a lot of paper. Where do we start?"

"Grab that notebook and start writing. I'll sort this stuff and tell you names to write as I go through. When we have a list, I'll figure out who to call first."

We worked until we had ten names of possible contacts, and the files were more or less organized into six piles. I dialed the numbers on the list. The first four were business numbers so I expected them to be closed. The next five went straight to voice mail. I left messages to call me back at all of them. The last number was out of service.

"Okay, so we wait," I said.

"There's a lot of waiting in this investigation stuff. I know what we can do, let me enter this stuff in your computer." Val cleared a space for my laptop. "Give me the password."

"Yeah, not likely." I started up the laptop and opened Outlook. "Don't screw up anything, please."

She laughed and started typing.

"I'll make us some dinner." I pulled a box of pasta from the cupboard and then froze. I heard the front door open, my throat closed. Peter? Jag? I turned and saw Jake.

"I need to talk to you. Can you come over?" He jerked his head toward the door.

TWENTY-TWO

I left Val to her organizing and followed Jake to his house. He didn't say anything until we were sitting in his living room facing a wall of windows, the mountains looming in the distance.

"Wow, I'm impressed at how fast you got your place cleaned up," he said as he put a plate of antipasto in front of me.

I tried to put aside my urge to rush him because I didn't want to fight again. "Oh, who told you how bad it was?" Like I had to ask.

"The lovely Delores. I was on a shoot all night and I just got your message. I hear it was a mess and a half. I'm glad to see you didn't leave it that way. I hate it when you wallow."

"Wallow?" I tried to feel insulted but he was right, I preferred a little mess to spending time on housework. "Okay, even I couldn't leave it in that shape." I decided to leave out the mention of professional help. Okay, more than help.

He laughed. "I have some news. Today's shoot was my last on the show. I'm heading out of town for a role in a movie."

"What happened? I thought you had a long-term part on that new TV show, what was it called?" I could never keep track of the Hollywood North news. There was always a movie or a series filming around town. Vancouver has been everything; a small American town, an alien planet, and even Vancouver.

"The Corner Cafe, well that was the working title. They decided my character needed to die in the first episode, so I'm gone." He sipped the wine. "It's weird, though, I was supposed to in the first four episodes with an option for the full season if it got picked up. This morning the director handed out the new scripts and my character had died in a car accident overnight. All I had to do was fill in the flashbacks."

I thought that was suspicious timing. "I'm sorry. I know you were looking forward to working with that crew again. Have you seen any new faces around the set in the last couple of days?"

Maybe this was a way into Jag's world. If he had his hands in the local movie industry, I would have an easier time getting someone to talk. Just because Jake was out didn't mean his friends wouldn't help. Secrets in the entertainment business were currency. They lasted as long as it took someone to call their favorite gossip columnist.

"I haven't noticed anyone." Jake split open a dried fig and stuffed a chunk of Brie inside. "Ed, remember my agent? He acted weird when he opened an envelope from Xiang Investments. As if it was a threat or something. That's the only weird thing I remember seeing, although the definition of weird is kind of loose in our business."

I laughed. "Remember that actor who used to come in and have the sets exorcised before he'd work?"

Jake's grin warmed me up. "Yes, but that's acting normal in our business, not weird."

My attention wandered as Jake took another bite and I fantasized about kissing that muscle I could see working on the side of his jaw. Damn my battered face. "So, where are you headed, and when?"

"I have to leave for the airport in a couple of hours. I'll be flying to Amsterdam tonight and then to Morocco tomorrow." He noticed my gaze on his jaw and leaned over to caress my swollen lip with his fingertips. "How are you feeling?"

"I'm healthy enough." I grabbed his shirt collar and pulled him closer. "I can kiss gently."

"Mmm, so can I."

"Why Morocco?" I asked as he leaned in for the kiss.

"There's a movie filming there." He kissed me before adding, "I've got a bit part." He brushed my lips again. "My agent thinks the part might grow."

He stood and pulled me up so we could move to his bedroom, then he carried me upstairs – very romance novel.

From his bed, we could see out across the marina. We didn't spend much time admiring the view. Instead we spent a blissful hour exercising the benefits part of our friendship. I took the opportunity to gather a few memories to keep me warm while Jake was away.

Just when I was settling in for a long cuddle, he stretched and kissed the top of my head. "I've really got to go, Charity."

I kissed him all the way to the front door. He hadn't bothered to get dressed, so we used the door as a privacy screen, his head poking around to say goodbye.

"I have to go." He kissed me again. "I have to shower, pack, and leave in the next half hour."

I guess I could understand why he wanted to get cleaned up before a nine or ten-hour flight. "I know." I let go of his hand and threw him a kiss. "Have fun in the desert."

"It's not a desert movie." He laughed and gave me that grin again.

"Okay, have a good flight and act your heart out. Don't forget to call me." I ran back to my place. He would be safe there, but I would miss him, and I realized it was more for his company than his body.

Val was waiting for me when I got back.

"Feeling relaxed?" She kept her eyes on the screen of my laptop.

"Yep. Thanks for asking." My home looked even more depressing after the color and vibrancy of Jake's. "Let's get out of here. I can't stand this. We can go for dinner on Robson."

"Is Jake joining us, or did you wear him out?" She typed something in the Google search bar. "I thought you might stay over."

"Yeah, well, I wouldn't just leave you here. He's going out of town." I stood behind her to see what she was surfing.

She closed the browser.

"What were you searching?"

"Nothing." She emptied the cache. "Let's go. I feel like sushi."

I picked up my purse. Clearing the cache meant I wouldn't be able to look in the history to see where she'd been surfing. "Am I going to find all kinds of spyware on my computer?"

"Nope." She stood at the open door waiting for me. "Come on. I'm hungry."

"No." I was getting suspicious. "Were you looking for some information on the gang?"

"A bit." She leaned against the door with her arms crossed. "I didn't find much. You probably found it already."

"What did you find?" I could feel ice fill my stomach. If she started to investigate on her own, Jag might find out and think it was me.

"That there's nothing to find on the Internet." She shrugged. "Come on."

"So, what else were you looking at?"

"Why's Jake leaving?"

It looked like she was willing to avoid answering forever. I decided to let it go, for now. "He got a part in a movie."

"What about that show he was on?" she asked, standing on the finger dock.

"His character dies. It happens." I locked the door.

"Yeah. It happens when Jag Chen gets involved."

WHILE WE WERE AT DINNER, my phone rang. The first call was from the furniture company confirming delivery sometime between eight and noon tomorrow.

"Great," I said to Val. "I guess we'll be stuck inside for the morning."

"Don't sweat it." She picked fries off my plate. "These are great. I'm glad the sushi place was full. Anyway, at least you'll have furniture. We can try to contact those people from your files if they don't call back."

"Shit, I meant to call them again, at least the personal numbers. I'll do it now." I wiped my fingers on the napkin and picked up my cell phone. I pulled the list of numbers from my pocket.

Then I decided to start with Lu. I was worried about her, it wasn't normal for her to be out of contact this long. I pressed the speed dial for her home number, it got through the first ring and then the call waiting beep happened.

I pressed the talk button. "Hey," I answered with my all-purpose greeting.

"Hey, yourself," Lu's voice came back like she was in a tunnel or something. The relief I felt made me realize how worried I'd truly been.

"Where are you?" I realized I was shouting, as if she couldn't hear me because I had difficulty making out her voice against the background noise. "Why haven't you been picking up your messages?"

"Who is it?" Val's question drowned out Lu's response. I shook my head at her hoping she would realize I needed to listen. "What?"

"I said, I've been busy, and you didn't say it was urgent." Lu's voice was almost drowned out in the background sound.

I guess I hadn't been as freaked out as I thought when I left the message. "I thought someone had done something to you."

"Oh, come on it hasn't been that long. We talked what, a day ago. What's the deal?"

"It's been almost two days. I got broken into and I—"

"You got broken into. Why didn't you call?"

"I did and left a message. Never mind. Look, can you get somewhere quieter or with better reception?" I lowered my voice because I noticed the glares of people at other tables.

Val mouthed, "Lu." and raised her eyebrow.

I nodded.

"No, I can't. I'm at a cocktail reception for the mayor," Lu shouted back. "I'm not actually on the phone while he's making his speech, I'm in the hall. I didn't want this information to wait. Can you talk?"

"Okay, go ahead," I pulled the pad of paper from my bag. If she'd stepped out of the presentation to call me, it was guaranteed to be good.

"Hang on. I'll go a bit farther down the hall. It will be quieter there." She lowered her voice as the background noise dropped off. "I called in some favors in the last couple of days. One of them just texted me with a time when the next shipment will arrive."

"Shipment of women?"

"What is she saying?" Val asked. I frowned and shook my head at her.

"Yeah, what did you think?" Lu said.

"Great, when and where? We can get the police on-site, and they can arrest everyone." I held my pen poised and ready to record the vital information.

"No!" It sounded like an order, like sit! "You need to know that I'm not a hundred percent sure about this person. It's a friend of a friend of an acquaintance kind of thing. If it's not legit, you'll lose any credibility you have left with the police."

Damn, I knew it had sounded too good to be true. "Okay, don't worry we'll go to plan B." Like I knew what plan B was.

"What plan B?" Val asked. I shushed her. It was hard to focus on Lu with the questions from across the table.

Lu said, "I didn't know we had a plan B."

She knows me too well. "What about an anonymous tip?"

"Jag will assume it's you. God knows what he'll do if he thinks you dragged him into court, and he gets off."

I could hear her tapping her fingers on the back of the phone. Gotta love the girl, looks like a hip ice queen, but fidgets up a storm when she's distracted.

"Give me the details and I'll think of something," I said with way more confidence than I felt.

"Okay, in two days at ten pm. They'll deliver a container of people to a warehouse held in the name of Y. Su Holdings. Charity, be careful." Her voice dropped to the point where I couldn't hear her. I guess the hallway of a hotel during a political event wasn't the most sensible place to be passing on information of a sensitive nature.

"I will. Go back to your party." I folded the phone shut.

"What did she say?" Val looked ready to jump across the table. I gave her a quick rundown of the news.

"We have to go look." She pushed her plate away.

"Slow down. We have two days. I need to get some information first, like the address of the warehouse. Let me make some more calls."

TWENTY-THREE

The next morning, my house started the transformation from an empty shell into a home again. The furniture and electronics arrived almost at the same time. It meant that the new TV and assorted add-ons had to be put out of the way until the entertainment stand was put up.

"Bedroom," I said and pointed upstairs when presented with a box labeled night table. Val was trying to shove boxes out of the way of the bigger pieces while the burly guy with the tats on his neck and arms hefted the new sofa bed with the help of the equally burly and pierced woman.

My cell buzzed in my pocket and I stepped out to the finger dock to answer it.

"Hey, Guy." It was my biker contact. Last night I had left more messages for Leigh, Guy, and an old contact who worked on the docks. So far Guy was the only one to call back.

"What did you need?" His social skills were limited when it came to small talk.

"I'm working on a story about crime levels in the areas around the docks."

"Why do you think I can help you with that? I can't talk to

you for long, it's not considered cool to talk to the press, you know."

Yes, I knew. Guy thought I was a journalist and had helped me with a case involving lost merchandise. In return I'd steered his niece away from a few bad choices.

"Do you know anything about a warehouse owned by Y. Su. Holdings?" I breathed in the sea air and felt the cobwebs clear from my lungs and head.

I heard a motorcycle engine rev in the background as Guy said, "There are lots of warehouses around here."

I noticed an otter floating on her back a few feet away from me. I tried not to believe she was sizing up my newly repaired floats as a mid-morning snack. "I don't care about the other warehouses. Can you tell me about the Y. Su one?"

"No," he snapped. "At least nothing I can give you. Stay away from it. Those people are dangerous."

"What, too dangerous for you?" I was half joking. The Hells Angels were serious bad asses, if they thought Jag's gang was dangerous, then I should probably think twice about what I was doing.

"No. At least not right now. We're working with them. I don't know how much of a choice we had, but I don't like it when I have to deal with them. You should back off."

"I know all about no choices." I waited, but he didn't respond. I was going to have to ask outright. "I have no choice about finding this place. Can you tell me where the warehouse is?"

"Look, you took care of Annie, so I'm going to keep you safe. So, my answer is no."

"Fine, I'll find out some other way. Tell Annie, hi from me."

"Wait."

I wasn't feeling good about it, but guilt usually worked on people, no matter how hard assed they were.

"You'll get into more trouble digging around for that company, or driving around looking. It's on Pandora and Victoria. There's a sign on the building, Sun Imports." He hung up.

Val and I spent the rest of the day planning our attack. She convinced me to allow her to come for the trip to reconnoiter, but I think I won the battle to keep her home for the actual event. We'd see how it worked when we got there.

TWENTY-FOUR

The next morning, we did some shopping for tools of the trade: black tee shirt, black jeans, black socks, black runners, red underwear, a voice recorder, and a new memory card for my camera. I decided not to rely on the all-purpose PDA. More equipment equaled more confidence in the quality. At least in my mind it did. The last thing I needed was to have grainy pictures, and fuzzy voice recordings.

We didn't have the details worked out for the big take-down, but I figured that would happen after we looked the place over and saw how I could get in

"Do you think Emma will be there?" Val kept her eyes on the streets we drove past.

"I don't know. I hope so. If she is, I get her out." I really did hope Emma was there, because if she wasn't I didn't have a clue where to look next.

It didn't take us long to get to Pandora and Victoria, but it was dark when I turned left off Hastings. The darkness would make it easier to skulk around, but harder to blend in because very few people hung out in this neighborhood after the streetlights came on. I was glad Val was with me. This was not an area I wanted to be in alone at night.

I drove around the block first to make sure I knew which building was the warehouse I needed. Then I parked next to a closed store on Hastings and Victoria. We walked the block downhill to Pandora and checked out the building. It looked innocent enough. Well, it looked like a warehouse and wasn't lit with a big sign saying, *evil done here.*

The sense of silence was so deep, that the sound of the rain dripping off the broken gutter of the warehouse roof was like applause. I felt like I was in the middle of a movie and the ax murderer was about to jump me. My shoulders twitched with the creepiness.

"I need you to keep an eye out for anything suspicious," I said to Val.

"There's no one here." She swept her arm around. "Let me come with you."

"I won't be long. If anyone comes—"

"Should I whistle?"

"Yes. Then get back to the car."

She sighed and leaned against the side of the end building in the row of warehouses across the street.

I walked around the building to get an idea of what entry points were available. The only door was in the front and it was solid, no gaps, and no wiggle room. There was a broken window on the second floor that might be useful. And a big blue dumpster underneath, which would get me in what looked like arms' reach of the sill. I didn't think there was much chance anyone would fix the window overnight so it was my first choice.

I checked, and Val was still standing where I left her. I started toward her and stubbed my foot on an uneven chunk of pavement. The city maintenance team hadn't been on this end of Hastings for years. The majority of the buildings were warehouses, like the one I had to break into. Of the others, some had retail sales areas, but it was that industrial style, no frills, and concrete floors. There were no lights in the buildings and a few of the streetlights were burned out.

I returned to Val. "Do you know who usually works these streets? It's kind of deserted. I don't know if that's normal."

"It's too early. Right now, the clients are with their families. Business around here is done during lunchtime and after dinner." She shrugged and headed for the car.

I felt in need of comfort food. "Speaking of dinner, let's walk up to Hastings and grab a pizza."

As we got closer to the buzz and hustle of this end of Hastings Street, I started to feel less bleak about what I was going to do. We found a bright restaurant and sat at a window table. There was a family of what looked like three generations sitting near the kitchen. They were passing food back and forth, laughing and yelling. I just wanted to pull my chair up and join them.

"When you find Emma, what will happen to her?" Val played with the ice in her soda.

"What do you mean?"

"I mean, will the police want to charge her with being a hooker?"

I didn't answer until the waitress had dropped our pizza and plates and left. "I don't think so. I think Leigh will be more interested in getting information on Jag than charging you or Emma with solicitation."

"It will be dangerous to talk about them." She cut the pizza apart and took a slice.

She was right. If Emma was anything like Val, though, I wouldn't be able to keep her from testifying. "Unless we catch them in the act, someone will have to talk." I cut a slice for myself. "It will take guts."

"Emma has guts to spare." She chewed the pizza.

"Really? You don't talk much about her. She's just a missing person to me."

"I like to think about the future. The past is done. Whatever we did before is over." Her words sounded practiced. I was sure she'd heard that somewhere and hung onto it to help put aside her present.

At least now she was being a real teenager. That whole 'I can survive anything' attitude they have. "Okay, but if you don't think Emma will be too afraid to talk, it will still be dangerous. I can't guarantee Jag and Peter will be off the streets – and they have friends."

"She won't be too afraid. She's really strong."

"Good." I tried to sound like I believed her.

"No, I am serious." Val picked cheese strings from the second slice of pizza on her plate. "She was on the wrestling team at school."

"Really? That's cool. I've never met a female wrestler before."

"Yeah." Val seemed to forget her reluctance to talk as she warmed up to her subject. "She kicked some ass in the competitions, too. She had tons of medals and stuff. She looked after me and my friends too. When you get her away from them, we're going to leave the streets."

What a difference from that thorny kid who banged on my door. "She sounds like a great big sister. What do you think you'll do?"

"Yeah, no one messed with us when she was around. I got some ideas about what we'll do." Val wiped her mouth on a napkin and looked around. "I gotta pee. Back in a minute."

It must be nice to be so young and willing to believe things will get better. I just hoped we would find Emma and she'd be in good shape.

TWENTY-FIVE

"I could keep watch for you," Val said. "You can't just go in there without back up."

We were getting ready for my assault on the warehouse. I was dressed in my new dark clothes, and we were filling my backpack with equipment.

"I need you here so I can call for help if need be." I checked my camera and the voice recorder before I put them in. "If you're near the warehouse, they might see you and then you'll be in danger. I need you out of danger."

She checked the battery life on my cell phone and then handed it to me. "I put the numbers you'll need in speed dial. Leigh is on number one. The house number is on speed dial two. You only need those. I also locked it on vibrate. Make sure it's on something soft. I also set your camera so it wouldn't make noise or flash."

"Thanks. I'll put the phone on my backpack when I get there."

"Are you sure you are ready for this?" Val started to sound like a big sister. I knew she was worried about Emma, but I was beginning to suspect she was worried about me.

I nodded and said, "Yes. I have all the equipment. I am prepared to wait all night if I have to. I know how to dial the speed dial."

She put a bag of trail mix into the backpack and added a purse pack of Kleenex. "You don't need water, but you'll need something to keep your energy up."

I was touched. "You've really thought this out."

"Yeah. Well. I need you to be able to get Emma out if she's there." She dug around in her pockets. "Here, if you get thirsty this will help."

I took the roll of mints from her. "I will be fine. You don't need to worry."

"Yeah, I know." Her voice cracked. "Look, I kind of like you, don't get any more beaten up, okay?"

I swallowed the lump in my throat. I knew how hard that must have been for her to say. "I'll try. That's all I can promise. Can I count on you to be safe here?"

"I swear. I'll be here waiting for the phone to ring." She shoved her hands into her pockets.

I tried to think of something more to reassure her. "Mike gave me some advice before he left." She shrugged again. "He used to be in private security, Val. I'm pretty sure he knows what he's talking about."

"What did he tell you?"

"He said to be careful, and to make sure I figured out an exit strategy. That's why I'm going in so early. I'll make sure I can get out if I have to."

She rolled her eyes. "Yes, and if I was there, maybe pretending to be working. I could help you get out, if it comes to that. I could call the cops, or maybe get some of the other girls to do something."

She was not going to let this go. I had to think of a way for her to accept she had to stay at home. "If you did that, you would look suspicious if you didn't get in a car with a client. I really need to know you are safe. If I am worried about where you are, I won't be able to keep my mind on staying quiet."

I pulled her into a hug. She stayed stiff for a second then softened into it and squeezed me back. As she pushed me away again she said, "Okay, I'll stay here. Don't get so mushy."

I grabbed my backpack. "I promise it will be all right."

I was making too many promises I didn't know how to keep.

THIRTY MINUTES LATER, I stood on tiptoes on the blue dumpster and my fingers could just grip the window ledge. That didn't mean I could use my fingertips to pull me up. My superpowers were in my other pants. I needed a new approach. I let go of the ledge and crouched down on the top of the dumpster to lower my profile while I looked around and thought.

The rain had stopped an hour before I left my house, but everything was wet and slippery. So, climbing was out of the question; I didn't need to lose my grip midway through a climb up the brick wall. I'd make a lot of noise even if I didn't get seriously hurt.

I wiped my hands on the seat of my jeans, and mulled over a new entry point. From here, all I could see was the drainpipe. Even if I could shimmy up the pipe, I'd get soaked and dirty. I wouldn't be able to lie still for very long in that condition. I suppose I could have done a better job of casing the joint last night. I'd stopped when I saw the window and hadn't considered a plan B. I really have to work on my contingency planning skills.

It was time to get a better look at the possibilities. I jumped down from the dumpster and walked around the corner of the building, keeping close to the side. I glanced up as I turned the corner, looking for any kind of security device. Not surprising for the rundown area, there was none. The building was completely detached from its neighbors, which was unusual for this block, most buildings shared a wall.

I could make my way around all sides of the warehouse. It was a tight squeeze between buildings, but I could get through. In my journey around the building, I saw four more broken windows, all higher than the first one and no handy ladders lying in the dirt, or ropes hanging to the ground. It was like the universe was trying to stop me from taking up breaking and entering as a career.

So, I was back to the original plan, get through the broken window. I needed some height. About four inches would make enough difference. I knew there was nothing in my car to help. I don't usually need to get taller while I'm out. The only other place I could think of was inside the dumpster. Even if I could get in, I'd come out more pungent than would be good for hiding.

I figured I had another twenty minutes before I had to be inside, or give up on the idea. And I had promised Val I'd get Emma out, so as long as there was a chance she'd be there, giving up wasn't an option.

I had enough time to look around the back alleys for a crate or something else I could stack on the dumpster. If I didn't find anything, I'd take my chances inside it. Before I ran to the first alley I checked to see if anyone was watching. One girl, maybe about sixteen, dressed in a micro skirt, four inch heels, halter top, and umbrella leaned against the building opposite. She didn't seem too concerned with me. I tried not to think about what put her on the streets.

I crossed over and ran down to the alley behind a row of businesses, a food processing plant, a box store, and a Mexican furniture import warehouse. I lucked out. There was a stack of ten wooden flats laid against the back of the food place. It would only take three to give me the extra inches I needed.

It was hard to manhandle three at once, but I didn't want to make repeat trips. I stuck my arms through the spaces in the wood frames and then bent my wrists up to form a hook. I scuttled back to the dumpster banging my shins with every step. Damn I was going to be bruised tomorrow.

The girl was still standing there. Her gaze followed me as I crossed to the dumpster. It was weird though, her attention seemed to be on something else, something internal. There were no cars cruising by yet, but it wouldn't be long before the customers, and other girls, would be start showing up.

I put the flats on top of the dumpster one at a time, then climbed up and stacked them one on top of the other. I stepped on the top of the whole construction. A bit wobbly, but it would hold and it was high enough.

I could see over the window ledge into the warehouse. I really had to act. I needed time to get inside and hide in the next five minutes so I could settle before the main event. I pulled the sleeve of my hoodie over my hand, pulled the rest of the broken glass shards out of the window, and dropped them down to smash on the street. When the frame was clear, I pulled myself up and looked inside before I leaped – for a change.

There was a metal grate below me, close enough to make it a good landing place. It was the top of a series of cages. I dragged myself halfway through the window and then managed to turn around and drop feet first onto the grate. Then I jumped to the floor. The landing made me gasp as the jolt echoed in my, not quite healed, jaw.

It was dark. I stood with my eyes closed for thirty seconds to let them adjust to the dimness. When I opened them again, the light from the street was enough to be able to see around the room.

I checked my watch. I had about ten minutes to settle in if I was right in my guess that Jag and Peter would show up early to get ready for the shipment.

I looked around. One wall was taken up with three metal cells, each with a bucket, a table, and four bunk beds. The other wall had an office and a staircase. I needed a place to hide, and an exit strategy. I saw a pile of boxes in one corner and checked them out. I could hide behind them but there was no line of sight to the rest of the room. And I would be trapped if they discovered me.

The staircase led to a walkway that ran around three of the walls. I could lay on the walkway and I would be able to see everything. But I would be visible to everyone. Time was running out. If they came in now I was dead, nowhere to run and nowhere to hide, no way to help Val and Emma.

My mind was running too fast for me to absorb the information. I stopped franticly glancing around and closed my eyes. After a count of a hundred to calm down, I opened them and started looking slowly around.

I stared at the top of the office. It was just below the walkway and had a raised edge I could hide behind. I sprinted up the stairs and along the walkway. The railing was hip high and easy to swing over. Before I lay on the roof, I remembered to look for the escape route Mike had insisted I have. There was a window along the back wall. If I needed to, I could get back on the walkway and jump through the window before anyone got up the stairs.

I pulled my cell phone out of the small backpack and pressed the speed dial for Leigh. I got her voicemail again. Fuck!

We'd had a chance to talk this afternoon, and she'd sworn she'd be available. I hadn't told her my plans, just that I'd need her tonight. I left a message to be ready when I called, but not to call me because my phone would be off. Then I turned it off, I didn't want to take the chance that it would vibrate itself off the backpack and call attention to me.

I lay face down and placed my voice recorder on the inside of the ledge. I would press record as soon as any action started.

Flattening myself on the office roof, I wiggled until I was in the most comfortable position I could find. It left a few blind spots, but I could see all the cages and most of the floor space. Just as I finished fussing, the front door screeched open.

I turned on the recorder.

"Get the blankets out of the office. They'll be here in half an hour and I don't want to hang around. This place depresses me." Jag's voice carried well through the empty building. I was sure my recorder would catch it all.

"How many in this shipment?" Peter was voice number two.

I realized my blind spot included most of the entrance to the warehouse when I noticed there was someone else in the building. I could see two shadows dancing around the walls as Peter and Jag prepared for the women. One shadow stayed still, the only movement was a twist of the head as whoever it was followed the movements.

Jag answered, "Twenty paid and got on. Probably some loss in transport but I haven't heard how much. I'm sure it will be in the usual range." He laughed. "If there's too many gone we'll take it out of the captain's share."

Oh my God, they were talking about these people as if they were merchandise. I gritted my teeth to stop from screaming. I had to stick it out and get the evidence.

"Get some buckets filled with soapy water," a woman's voice called. I guess this wasn't just an old boy's gang. "I can't stand the stink of them when they get here."

I didn't recognize the voice. I knew it wasn't Mary, but that's all I could tell. I couldn't take the chance and peek because it had become so quiet they would have heard me shift.

I'd look later, when there were more people and some cover noise.

There was the sound of footsteps on the concrete floor, a whispery, gritty scrape from the dust. Peter and Jag moved into my line of sight. Well, at least, their heads did. I noticed that Jag had styled his hair to cover a large bald spot on the crown.

I could see Peter throwing blankets in the cages. He didn't bother to put them on the beds, just threw them on the floor. Jag put a couple of white plastic bags on each table. It looked like take-out. A circular red logo was on the side of each bag. The plastic of the bags was molded to the round and rectangular shapes inside. Jag moved out of my line of sight, and then returned with large jugs of water and placed them beside the bags.

"Who's on babysitting tonight?" The woman again. She was staying by the door and I couldn't see her at all.

"Hong, he's only on tonight. This group will be out of here and working by tomorrow." I watched Peter pull a phone out of his pocket. He was standing in the center of the room. And I could see all of him, from shining black shoes all the way up his European black suit to his spiked head of hair. "What? Okay." He clicked it shut. "Ten minutes. Four of them didn't make it."

"Okay, that's within what we expected." Her voice was flat and businesslike.

I pictured some kind of evil stepmother type. I really needed to get a look at her to make sure I could identify her. I hadn't been able to get in position to take a picture yet. As soon as the women arrived, I'd take the chance and wiggle over to get a look, and maybe a picture.

"It's ready." Peter came back from the corner where he had been filling buckets with water from a tap in the wall. He put four buckets in the center of the room and then dragged over a big garbage can. Jag appeared with his arms full of gray clothes. Tee shirts and track pants by the look of it.

"What are you going to do about that stupid girl who's been snooping?" She was talking about me. I stopped planning how I would peek, and started listening.

"You don't think she's smart enough to take the warning?" Peter called it a warning. I called it a threat. "I haven't seen her around since I went over to her place."

"She hasn't been back to the restaurant. Maybe she's backed off."

Oh my god. She knew I'd been to see Winnie. If Lu hadn't been able to get her away, I hate to think what I had exposed her to. I added taking care of Winnie to my mental list of things to do after I catch Jag and Peter.

"I guess we'll find out. If she has backed off, we won't see her around. If we see her around, then she won't see us coming." Jag gave a wheezy cackle.

The woman asked the question that was burning in my mind. "Will you follow through on the threat I told you to make?"

"What kill her friends?" Jag's shadow shrugged. "I guess if that's what you want. Why wouldn't we just kill her and be done with it? Killing her friends seems too complicated, too likely to cause someone to snoop around. Too Russian Mafia."

"The Russians didn't invent it," she snapped. "You know damn well if we don't punish her before we kill her there will be repercussions from the top. What makes you more scared, the boss or the cops?"

Jag's answer was immediate, "The boss, no question."

"Well. Then you'll kill her friends and make sure she knows how they died. It better be bad. Then you kill her, slowly. If Hong Kong finds out you didn't, they'll start with your son, then your wife. And you live a very painful week regretting your kindness."

Damn, I know in my head that women can be as bloody-minded and cruel as men, but in my gut, it seemed worse. Even now, when I knew from my research, the biggest ringleader of snakeheads in the world was a woman. I just hope Leigh got my message and was on her way with the modern-day equivalent of the cavalry.

Headlights spilled white light through the open door. I heard someone moving to greet the driver. The engine of the vehicle outside was too loud to be a police cruiser coming to the rescue. It rumbled roughly even though it must be idling, a diesel truck by the depth of the sound.

Two people were talking outside. I couldn't hear the words over the engine noise, but I could tell it was two men. I heard the sound of a roll-up door open and a ramp screech down and thump on the road.

TWENTY-SIX

The engine outside rumbled on but there was no other sound for a few seconds. Then a new head moved into my line of sight, then another. The women walked to the center of the room, heads down, shoulders rounded, feet shuffling. They looked to me like every ounce of hope and humanity had been drained from them. They had been turned into merchandise in their minds as well as in the minds of these snakeheads.

I heard the sound of the truck ramp going back and then the door being rolled down. The rumble of the engine changed, and the truck drove away.

Jag told the women to strip and wash. Peter had to interpret. They obeyed in silence. I heard the drip and splash of the water as they wet the cloths in bucket. The quiet was peaceful, if you could forget the reason for the sound. I found myself drifting off, thinking about my parents and how my friends had helped me.

Jag's laugh snapped me back to my senses.

I looked down at the women huddled in the center of the room. They didn't have anyone to phone, no one to sit with them, and make them feel there was hope in the future. They couldn't even talk to each other.

What difference would it make if they could talk? You need someone who isn't in the same boat to help you learn to swim.

I carefully turned my wrist to check my watch. Forty minutes had passed since I crawled through the window. My recorder had another hour of capacity before it stopped working, which should be enough. I didn't think the three of them would hang around that long. I hoped Leigh would get here before they left.

I turned my focus back to the slice of warehouse I could see. It was dangerous to be inattentive here. I reminded myself if I made a noise, it would end badly for everyone. Getting caught by Jag and Peter would be death for me, my friends, and probably these women too.

The women had finished washing and were waiting for their next set of instructions. I saw towels being thrown at them from out of my line of sight.

I started making plans B and C while I watched. If Leigh didn't get here before Jag and his people left, I'd call Lu. She'd have some connections. Someone who could take these women in for a while. I'd just take care of getting them out. With the mystery man coming to babysit, there wouldn't be any unsupervised time to just run down and open the door. No problem. I'd call Val and tell her to call 911. I just needed some cover for a whispered conversation. I'd split the women up between my place, Jake's, and Mike's. Then I would find Leigh and make her help me.

My hip had started hurting a half hour ago, and now my back was starting to spasm. All the new pains reminded my body that I hadn't healed from the beating, so my jaw started joining in and throbbing in tune with my pulse. It was too quiet for me to move, but if I didn't get some cover noise soon, I'd be stuck in this position for a long time.

"Finish drying," Jag shouted at the women. They were standing in a loose group, holding the towels.

"They don't understand. Shout louder." Peter laughed as though he'd made the funniest joke in the history of jokes.

"Move," Jag shouted again.

I needed to see more of what was going on. Watching these women wasn't helping. They were so deep in shock that they barely reacted to anything.

"Move, damn it." Jag said again.

I heard a thud. I couldn't contain my need to see more, and it might be time to start taking pictures. I stretched to peek over the edge of the building. A few inches increased my field of vision to most of the floor, and I saw one of the women lying down. She must have been pushed.

Peter stepped into sight and started shoving women into the cages, pulling the towels away as they came into reach.

Jag kicked the woman on the ground as she tried to stand. Her legs wouldn't support her so she crawled over the concrete floor to the nearest open cage.

Jag and Peter threw clothes in and slammed the doors shut.

"I'm starving," Jag said. "Let's get out of here." He turned away from the cage doors and looked right into my eyes. "What the fuck is she doing here?"

TWENTY-SEVEN

Jag was already running toward the staircase, the sound of his shoes on the concrete floor pounding through my head. I moved the voice recorder back a bit so it wouldn't be easy to see and be taken.

I tried to leap up like I'd pictured it when I planned my escape route earlier. The problem was I hadn't factored in the effect of my damaged body in the plan. I'd been lying on my belly for almost an hour. My neck and shoulders were strained from holding my head up so I could see. The small of my back was frozen in position.

I wasn't twelve anymore, so the bounce I imagined was more of a groan and struggle in reality.

I gritted my teeth, tightened my stomach muscles, and pushed myself up, trying to ignore the agony. It's amazing what panic can do to overcome pain. But by the time I got over the railing and headed toward that window, Jag was at the top of the staircase.

I pushed as much speed as I could into the run, focusing only on the window and ignoring where Jag was. I could only hope for the best, and concentrate on getting my body to make the leap.

I could see Peter on the floor. He stared at me and then ran to the front door, he would be there when I landed if I didn't move faster.

Why hadn't I thought about getting cut off when I found this stupid exit? *Okay, Charity, bend your knees and hit the ground running*, I told myself as I prepared to launch my body through the window.

I didn't get a chance to break my leg, or neck, in the jump. Jag grabbed my jacket and jerked me back just as I took off. His pull caused me to lose my balance and fall on the metal catwalk.

The pain felt like I'd added a broken rib to my list of injuries, assuming I lived to worry about injuries. The good news was that the adrenalin spike had dulled all my pains. I could feel them in the back of my mind, but in abstract. Fear took control of me. I didn't have anything left to fight back.

"Fucking bitch." He grabbed my arm and dragged me to the staircase. "Why don't you listen? What is so fucking important to you?" He was spitting his anger out with every word.

"I'm looking for office space." My fear-frozen brain wasn't smart enough to beg for mercy. Or, maybe, I was just too stubborn to let him see I was scared. Either way as long as we were talking I was alive.

He pushed me over the top step. I struggled to keep my balance, no need to do any more damage to the old body. I made it to the bottom of the stairs without a scratch. The front door was only three steps away. I tried to run for it, but Peter stepped around the wall and stood in my way.

I looked around for the mystery woman but she was gone. I guess she didn't want me to see her. Maybe she didn't like getting her hands dirty for all her hard talk. Maybe I knew her.

Could it be Mary after all? No, she'd threaten Jag's family, and I can't see the ice queen doing that.

Jag dragged me into the office and pushed me into a chair. "Shut the fucking door," he yelled at Peter then turned back to me. "You are going to be very sorry you didn't take our advice."

I looked up at him. "Yes, probably I am." I tried to put on a calm unconcerned air, as though it didn't matter what he did. "I usually end up regretting my impulses. But I never seem to learn to behave." I sighed. "Maybe one day, when I'm old and wise, I'll change." The sigh had burned through my lungs. I guess maybe I had broken something, but I wasn't going to let him know that.

"You think your friends are going to find this so funny." He slapped me and my mouth exploded in fresh pain. "That skinny bitch on the North Shore is going to regret it when we break her fingers. Your boyfriend isn't going to find it easy to get parts when we cut off his ears."

"Nice." I ignored the wave of grey that flowed over my vision. I wouldn't pass out, damn it! "Isn't that from that Tarantino movie? What was it called again? Oh, yeah *Reservoir Dogs*."

"You'll wish this was just a movie." He slapped me again, this time it just hurt rather than overwhelmed me.

"Peter, get your ass over here. I don't want to touch her any more than I have to."

"I don't think we should do it here," Peter said.

"What? You think those cows over there will talk? You think they are going to tell the police?" He smashed his fist against the wall. "I'll shut them up permanently, if I have even a hint they would look at a cop."

So much for an easy escape as they moved me. I hoped the recorder was getting this. Even if I didn't make it, Val would make sure someone checked for the equipment.

"Where's your gun?" Jag snapped his fingers at Peter.

"In the car," Peter said, turning to leave.

"Bring something to wrap her in." Jag leaned against the wall and smiled as he watched me. "It'll be messy. Get something watertight."

Peter turned back. "There's nothing in the car that will work for that. I'll get some garbage bags from the corner store."

"Make it fast." Jag looked up suddenly. "Wait, when is Hong coming?"

Peter checked his watch, "Soon. Why?"

"No reason. Just wanted to know if we would be sharing her with him. I guess not."

Peter shrugged. "No, unless you want to wait?"

"I'm starving, and I want to get home. We'll be done by the time he gets here."

With Peter gone, I might have a chance. Jag was so mad, maybe he'd get careless. Then again, I was also scared shitless, so we were about even.

There was noise from the women, but not enough to distract him. I guessed they could be screaming and he wouldn't be worried. I looked around for a weapon. I couldn't see much that looked useful, but I didn't have any experience with weapons, improvised or not.

There was the chair I was using, but it didn't seem heavy or pointy enough. Along the far wall, I saw a cheap metal desk, painted serviceable gray. If I didn't have a broken rib maybe I could throw it at him. The only other option was a big metal garbage can that stood in the corner across from where Jag leaned. It looked like the kind of thing that people used to hold garden clippings.

"How long have you been doing this?" I asked. Maybe if I kept him talking, I could make a dash for the door.

"Long enough." He crossed his arms and rolled his neck.

"You make me think it's too long in this town." He glanced through the window as more noise came from the women outside. "Stupid cows, what are they crying about?"

"Maybe they're just realizing they landed in hell." I kept my eyes on him and slid to the edge of the chair.

The door to the office was open and from where I was sitting, I could see through it to the front door. Peter had left it ajar. If I could move quickly enough, I could get through it. If I kicked the chair toward Jag, it would be between us, and maybe that would make the difference. A couple of seconds' lead was all I needed. If I got a break from the universe, he would trip over the chair and I'd have more than a few seconds.

"You think they didn't know that as soon as the door to the container closed in China?" He started laughing.

I shifted my weight in the chair and grabbed both arms tightly. The pain in my side stabbed to remind me I was holding my breath. I breathed out quietly through my nose.

Jag turned toward the window and started yelling at the women to shut up.

I launched my body doorward.

Behind me, I heard the metal legs of the chair screech against the floor and then bang into the desk. I heard Jag swearing, but it sounded a long way behind me. That could be the adrenaline, or shock, kicking in.

I knew that I would only get through the street door if I ignored the sounds behind me, Jag swearing, women crying. It would only work if I believed, believed that Jag was falling over the chair, and believed that my rib wasn't boring a hole in my lung.

I heard the women start to scream and I saw the door opening inward. I put my head down and wrapped my arms around my chest. I planned to ram right past Peter before he realized what was happening.

If my lung didn't explode, I might make it to the nearest streetlight.

TWENTY-EIGHT

It didn't work. I crashed into the person who was coming through the door. Thank god, I was smart enough to turn my body to the least damaged side. Then I realized I encountered softness rather than the hard muscle I expected. The person just grabbed me and turned with the motion. I opened my eyes and looked right into the green ones of my favorite police constable.

Leigh smiled and propped me against the side of the building, holding me until I got my equilibrium back. When she let me go, the world started to open up beyond my tiny one of pain.

I heard screams from inside, and then they got louder. I started to go back in to stop Jag from whatever he was doing.

Leigh gently pushed me back against the wall.

I pushed back. Okay it was feeble, but I couldn't stop and let the women suffer. "Jag's in there, he's hurting those women. Peter Wong, he's here somewhere, too."

Leigh increased the pressure on my shoulders. "Don't worry. We're on top of everything. Peter is in the car over there, and those two are waiting to get Chen." She pointed to two large heavily armed constables standing at the door. As I looked, they stepped forward and grabbed Jag who had just limped through. I noticed a long tear in his pant leg. Yay me!

More people went in, so I decided I could stop worrying.

"I got your message," Leigh said.

"Uh huh." I winced. My pains were all coming back with a vengeance. "Why weren't you calling me back? I was freaking out."

"I got all your messages. I didn't know how safe it was to call back. And then you said your phone was off."

I really wanted to yell at her, but I didn't have the energy. "There's a shipment of women in the warehouse. They are the only ones left inside."

"What do you mean, the only ones left inside? Why would there be anyone else, Chen and Wong are in custody." She paused for a second, but before I could answer she jumped to the right conclusion. "Was there someone else there?"

"A woman came in with them. She seemed to be calling the shots. Didn't you know that there was someone else in charge?"

"No. This is the first indication that Jag isn't number one." She nodded to the waiting cops and they went into the building.

"Look, I don't want to be a pain, but can you get an ambulance here? I think I've broken something." I could feel my legs give way as a film of sweat cooled on my body. I was about to pass out.

"Sorry, sorry." Leigh's voice came from a distance. "Al, get a couple of ambulances here. The women inside will probably need some care."

She helped me sit so I could avoid falling, and breaking something else. "Hang on it will be a couple of minutes."

"Okay." I breathed slowly to keep the pain under the threshold of scream. "I left a recorder on the top of the office roof. And my cell phone. I need to call Val."

"We'll get it, Charity. I don't know how much use the information will be." She lifted my chin so I was looking in her eyes. I guess she was trying to keep me conscious. "You broke into the warehouse which is technically a crime."

"Sorry." I didn't care about that. "Doesn't the fact that I'm a journalist following a lead make it okay to use the evidence I gathered?"

"Yes, it might work. But you're not really a journalist, are you? Why don't we let Crown Council figure that out?"

"You'll find enough on the recorder to tie those two to the people trafficking trade."

"Good." She made a few notes on her pad. "You getting beaten up and running from the building gives us sufficient reason to enter. Jag will get charged with assault at the least. Maybe one of them will turn on the gang."

I just nodded. My entire body was throbbing with pain, and I really needed to get taken care of. She handed me her phone and I called Val.

"I'm going to be fine. No. I'm sorry, Emma wasn't there. Don't worry. We'll find her. I have to go to the hospital. No. I'll be fine."

I could hear sirens approaching. It was the sweetest sound in the whole of my memory.

The paramedics approached, and Leigh stepped aside so they could take care of me. There were a few minutes of simple questions, and a couple of pokes, then I was put on the bed in the back of the ambulance.

They took me to VGH. Painkillers took me to sleep.

TWENTY-NINE

The next morning, the nurse handed me some Tylenol 3 to take and a prescription for more, and then told me I could go home. Nothing was broken, but I did have two cracked ribs, and enough bruises to make it painful to breathe, walk, talk, okay pretty much everything.

Lu and Val picked me up, and drove me to the police station to make my statement. Then I could go home and sleep.

"Are you going to rest after this?" Val asked.

"Probably." I pressed the button to let the traffic light gods know we wanted to cross. "But don't worry, we'll look for Emma tomorrow."

They waited in the lobby of the station while Leigh handed me my visitors pass and led me back into the office to make a statement. The whole thing seemed much tamer when I read over the written copy.

Leigh told me that the women were all put up in a hotel and would stay there until the court case, probably a year or two from now. They wouldn't have much freedom, but I figure it's better than what Jag planned. I hoped Lu could work out a way for them to stay before the authorities sent them back to China.

The whole process didn't take long. I was walking down the steps with Val and Lu before the Tylenol 3 wore off.

While we were waiting for the light to change, a woman walked toward us. She was familiar but I couldn't quite place her. She was dressed in this great chocolate pinstriped suit and four-inch maroon heels. Her cell phone matched her suit and she was yelling into it in Cantonese.

She didn't seem to be aware that there was anyone within listening distance.

I felt sorry for whoever was on the other end of the line. They were going to regret whatever it was they'd done to make her mad. She was clutching a cream and blue purse like it was the neck of a chicken she was killing for dinner.

I kept looking at the chocolate pinstripe woman, trying to drag the memory up from the depths of my brain. Her makeup was a bit too heavy for her age, like she was filling in the wrinkles with foundation. It didn't work.

Lu started to cross the street. I grabbed her arm.

I knew this woman. I just couldn't put a pin in where I'd seen her. I closed my eyes to block out the distractions.

"What's wrong?" Val patted my arm. "Do you need some painkillers?"

"Sh." I needed to concentrate. I couldn't see her and so all I had was the voice. Suddenly I was back in the warehouse.

It was the woman from last night. And I still had that feeling I knew her from somewhere else.

"That woman was there last night," I hissed at Lu as I turned to look. All I saw was the woman's back as she went through the doors of the station. "I know her from somewhere else."

Val drew me back from the intersection. "Okay, who are the Asian women you've met lately? I mean ones that weren't in chains."

"Not that many."

I ran through my memory of the last few days. The women from the art show didn't seem likely suspects. Except for Mary, they were all solid citizens.

Suddenly a face swam into my mind. "Oh my god." I grabbed Lu's arm. "It's Winnie."

"What?" Lu looked around, mouth open.

"The moles," I whispered.

"Moles? What the hell are you talking about?"

"The reason I recognized her, the three moles on her eyebrow. I saw them when I met her."

"I thought she was a victim," Val said. "You were all wound up about putting her in danger."

The questions started crowding my mind. "Yes. I don't know how we got sucked into thinking that. Although, now I think about it, why did she meet with us?"

Lu shook her head. "I don't know." She grabbed me as I turned back to the station. "You can't go back in there. She may not have noticed us before, but she won't be able to miss you in the station. She'll bolt, and then no one will be able to find her."

I called Leigh, got her voicemail, again. "There's a woman coming into the station, brown suit, red shoes and aggressive attitude. She's the woman from last night."

"Now what? We can't just leave it at that," Val said.

Lu laughed. "Well, we could, but I know Charity won't."

Val turned. "I'll go inside and check it out."

"No," Lu said. "It's too dangerous."

"She hasn't seen me. I'll be careful." Val ran to the station stairs before either of us could stop her.

"Go get the car," I said to Lu. "We'll want to follow her when she comes out."

. . .

WHEN SHE GOT BACK with the car, Lu double-parked and turned on her hazard lights. I slid into the back seat, leaving the passenger seat for Val so she could just jump in.

"Hey, see the hazards, asshole," Lu called to a driver who hadn't appreciated having to change lanes in heavy traffic.

"Lovely," I said. "Let's try to attract as much attention as possible."

Lu was watching the station entrance in her rear-view mirror. I turned to follow her gaze and saw Winnie stamp down the stairs right behind Val.

Val jumped into the passenger seat. "She was mad. The cops wouldn't let her see Jag. I thought she was going to throw a fit."

Lu was watching Winnie wave down a cab. "It looks like we're going mobile."

I called Leigh and left her another message, telling her to call my cell number.

We followed the cab along Cordova until it merged with Powell.

"Shit," I held onto the seat as Lu slammed on the brakes. We missed the light at the railway track.

Val leaned forward in her seat. "I can see them. They are stuck because a truck is turning left from the other side. See, the cab is right in front of that yellow Jeep."

"They'll be stuck there for a while," Lu said. "It looks like that truck is going to have to make a few adjustments before it will get around. Keep your eye on them."

Just as our light changed, the truck cleared the road and the traffic started moving again.

"Okay that was lucky." I leaned forward then sat back when the pressure of the seatbelt found the bruises on my chest. "Don't get too close, but don't lose them."

"I'm trying for crap sake." Lu switched lanes without signaling. "It's not that easy."

THIRTY

For the next few minutes, we dodged trucks and delivery vans, keeping two cars between the cab and us. We reached Victoria and turned right, the direction of last night's warehouse. I felt a surge of sickness fill my throat at the thought of going back.

We saw the taxi turn into an alley behind the Glenhaven Funeral Center as Lu drove past. We rounded the block and the taxi pulled out of the other end of the lane without his passenger. Lu parked the car and we sat there scoping it out.

"She must be in one of those places." I pointed to the three loading docks facing the Glenhaven parking lot.

"Probably the middle one," Val said.

"Why that one?" I asked. "We can't be jumping at guesses."

"I know," Lu said. "But the kid is right. Look, the first one is a retail store. Winnie can't be up to anything with all those people going in and out."

Val pointed. "Yeah, and the last one can't be it either. That guy on the loading bay doesn't look like a snakehead."

I had to agree with her. He had a gray ponytail and was wearing a collarless cotton shirt over faded blue jeans. By the look of the wood stacked on the loading bay, he was running a handmade furniture shop.

"Yeah. I guess it is likely to be the middle one," I said.

Lu poked me with her dragon red nails. "Call your buddy the cop, again. She needs to figure out how to get inside and find out what's going on."

I grimaced. "You do remember I'm hurt, right?"

"Yeah, yeah, call her," Lu said.

So, I followed orders and called Leigh. Again, with the voicemail. This was getting annoying. I get that she can't tell me what to do, but it would be nice just to have her say hello. I left a message telling her where we were, and that we'd wait until she got here, or Winnie left, whichever came first.

Val turned to look at Lu. "So how did you find this Winnie?" she asked, beating me to the question.

"I told Charity already. It was someone who volunteers at an organization I work with. I don't know how this happened. Maybe there was a real Winnie. Maybe this woman took her place." Lu poked me again. "I was trying to help you. You should have asked me sooner. I would have done better with more notice."

I rolled my eyes. "Oh, that's so helpful. Blame me for getting in the way of an international crime ring."

Lu poked me again. "Oh, yes, and you are such a Miss Innocent when it comes to screw ups."

"Who, me?" I fluttered my lashes. My pitiful tone got drowned in giggles. I held onto my sides to try to keep my ribs from tearing pain through my lungs. I couldn't control it. Stress does weird things to people. I guess laughter is really a fear response like they say. I looked at Lu and Val, and they had grins spread across their faces, and tears squeezing out of the corners of their eyes.

I looked down at my lap in an effort to get control. "Stop it.

It's not the right time for a laughing fit." And that's all I could get out before the giggles took control.

"Stop," Lu breathed out. "Don't look at me until I get this under control."

She was right, the only way to control this hysterical fit was to stop looking at each other until we calmed down. I tried to focus on watching the warehouse. It wouldn't be a good idea to miss seeing Winnie leave just because we were out of control. I forced my breathing to slow down, and finally the laughter stopped. I just couldn't look at Val or Lu.

My phone vibrated. I checked the ID, unknown number. "Yes."

"Charity," Leigh's voice cut through my barely controlled giggles. "Sorry, I was in the can when you called. I got your other messages, though. Where are you exactly?"

I gave her our location including the make, color, and license number of Lu's car.

"I'll be there in ten minutes. Don't do anything stupid."

That's so judgmental. I mean, really, what is stupid? Letting Winnie get away would be stupid. At least that's what I thought, what I said was, "Yes, we'll wait here for you."

TEN MINUTES LATER, Leigh and a second cruiser came around the corner, lights spinning but no sirens. We stepped out of the car to talk to her.

"She's in the middle building. Go get her." I thought it was worth a try.

Leigh stood on the sidewalk, apparently not ready to charge into the building on my order. "Okay. What do you think is going on in there?"

"I don't know, but I'm sure it's not a knitting circle."

She huffed. "I need more than your guess. I can't arrest her for being in a building."

"I'm sure you'll find something going on if you just go in." I was surprised that Lu and Val were so silent.

"Did you hear anyone screaming? Any shots fired? Does it look like there's a drug operation going on?" Leigh sounded accusing.

Okay. I guess I understood. I wouldn't want the police breaking into my house because someone told them something was going on. I just wanted her to do something for God's sake. "If the police can't do something, what can we do? I'm afraid she'll get away and start all over again in another city."

"You can go home. I'll keep her under surveillance. We'll follow her when she comes out. Maybe we'll get lucky."

Yeah. They'll follow her and by the time they get around to make an arrest, more women will have been fed into the machine of greed and heartlessness. It wasn't going to work for me. "Okay," I lied. "I want to be in on the arrest, and I want the story from your point of view."

"Still acting the journalist?" Leigh's eyebrow curved up.

"No. I'm not playing. I do write articles." I hadn't done it for a while, but I still knew how to get a byline.

"Just trust the process. I'll call you when we get her." Leigh pulled her phone out of her pocket. "I've got your number saved. I promise you'll get the exclusive."

"Thanks." Gee, I practically hand her the arrest and she'll keep me posted.

We got back into Lu's car and stared at each other for ten seconds.

"Emma might be ..."

"What were you...?"

They both started talking at the same time. I held up my hand.

"No, I'm not going to just crawl back into my safe house and wait for the police to come to the rescue. We've worked too hard to just let them step in."

"Good," Lu said.

"So what's the plan?" Val asked.

"I don't know. We need to get the cops in the building. I'm sure there's something going on." I could feel my gut twisting with tension. "If there are innocent people in there we need to make sure they are safe. If Emma's in there, we need to be able to get her out. I'm not sure. What do you think we should do?"

"I'm glad you aren't going to just rush in," Lu said. "Before you start dashing around, though, how are you feeling? You must be in pain from your ribs, at least."

"A bit but what does that have to do with anything?" I'd forgotten the pain in my urgency to catch Winnie.

Lu raised her eyebrow again before answering. "Any plan we have needs to take it into account. I assume you won't let either of us do anything but plan and support." She was always the practical one. It never seems to stop her from getting into trouble with me. She just made sure my plans were sensible enough to have some hope of success.

It didn't help me figure out a plan though. "I guess it's probably not enough for me to just run into the building and come out screaming."

"What if you snooped and saw something you could tell Leigh that will allow her to go in?" Val said.

"Okay. That's simple, but I think she'll need something more than me running toward her yelling, help police, evil being done here. Sorry, I know you are trying." My giggles were long gone, but my sense of humor was still in place.

"No, but you have a cell phone that takes pictures. What kind of phone does she have?" Val lifted her chin to indicate Leigh. I could see her on the radio, watching us.

"Same as mine. I guess that means she can look at any pictures I send. Now we have plan." I turned and pulled the seatbelt around me, gently this time. "Drive away, so she doesn't have a chance to stop us before we get what we need. Go toward the water and drop me off as soon as you turn the corner. I'll find a way to look inside. There's got to be something I can find that will let her go in."

Lu drove around the corner and stopped.

Val stared at me and started interrogating, "Are you sure you're up to this? How's your pain? Should Lu do this?"

"I'm fine. The pain's not too bad and I'll be careful. Besides, how would Lu get this done? She's wearing three inch stilettos."

"Hey. I didn't know I'd be called to action. A girl needs notice for stealth wear."

"Wish me luck." I opened the door and ran to the side of the building. Well I planned a run, but it was more of a fast limp.

Lu drove off and I found myself alone in another alley looking at another blue garbage container. The difference, other than the fact it was bright daylight, was that there were no broken windows just out of reach, no windows on the alley at all.

I slipped around the corner away from Leigh's line of sight. It looked like the only way I was going to get a picture was to go in through the front door right under Leigh's nose. I wasn't feeling too happy about that. And, for a change, I didn't just jump in feet first, eyes closed. I called Lu to get advice from my two partners in crime.

She told me to hold on and I could hear her talking to Val, but not what she was saying. While I waited, I watched the old hippie still on his loading bay. He hadn't noticed me, and I hoped it would stay that way. I was going to have to run past him to get to the open door of Winnie's place. I didn't need him to try to chat when I got into action.

"Okay," Lu got my attention back. "We'll drive back and stop in front of the cops. Then we'll get out and distract them while you run."

"She'll notice I'm not there."

"Yes, that's why you'll have to run."

"I guess it's going to work. By the time she notices me, it will be too late to stop me. I don't think she'll try to shoot me. Well at least not to kill."

"Let's hope you're right." Lu hung up.

THIRTY-ONE

I poked my head around the corner of the building and crouched low. I'd seen it often enough on TV, go in low so when someone shoots at head height they miss.

Leigh was sitting in her car.

As I watched, Lu pulled up right in my line of sight. That was my cue. I wrapped my arm around my ribs and ran to the door.

Just as I reached to open it, I heard Leigh shout. "Charity, stop right where you are."

I opened the door farther and stuck my phone in front of me snapping pictures as I went.

I didn't go all the way in, I didn't need to.

I checked to see that I'd got the pictures before spinning to run back to Leigh. The photo I held out in front of me was of four cages full of women.

"I told you to stop." Leigh grabbed the phone from me.

I ignored her reprimand and pointed to the pictures. "Is that enough information?"

"Yes. Good thing I called for the other car to come back when your friends pulled up."

Winnie came running out of the door fist raised as though she was going to punch me out. Leigh grabbed her, and used Winnie's own momentum to spin her against the wall.

The two solid blocks of muscle who followed Winnie went into the hands of two uniformed cops.

"You aren't going anywhere, lady," Leigh said while clipping the handcuffs on.

Leigh passed Winnie to one of the other cops, and told us to wait outside. It didn't work, Val pushed me aside and Lu followed her. I went in to make sure they didn't damage anything – at least, that would be my excuse.

It was hard to see what was going on in the room. There wasn't a lot of light, but what I could see was heartbreaking. There were rows of cages like a rabbit warren. They looked to be three by three feet. There were two women in each cage and all of them stared at us with blank looks.

"Emma," Val called as she ran along the cages. She looked into each one, then ran to the next. She disappeared around the corner before I could stop her.

"Charity, go after her," Leigh said. "We'll take care of this."

I ran to catch up with Val, hoping that Emma wasn't lying dead in one of the cages. I could hear Val's voice calling 'Emma', sounding more frantic each time.

The women in the cages must have realized they were going to be okay because they started making noise, crying, and calling out to whoever was opening the cages. I don't think Emma's voice would carry through the rising cacophony.

Val was running to the last row of cages when I caught up to her. I didn't stop her, I just waited for her to finish.

Emma hadn't answered.

"Damn, damn, damn." Val crumpled in the corner, sobs shaking her body.

I sat beside her and pulled her into my arms. "Okay. We'll

start looking again. Don't give up." I felt my bruises protested as she burrowed into my arms.

"I was sure she'd be here," she sobbed out.

"Me too. But she's not, and that's a good thing."

She pulled back and rubbed her face with her hands. "I guess. At least we didn't find her body, right? At least we didn't find her dead."

Small comfort, but she was right. "Wait until Leigh's done getting the women out. We'll just sit here for a while."

Lu joined us and we sat on the floor with our arms around each other listening to the women leave. I heard the cage doors clank open in the last row, and then Leigh stepped into view.

"Charity, come with me." She beckoned me to the far wall. I asked Val to wait and she just nodded.

Leigh reached up and grabbed a chain. Along with the chain came a set of stairs. I realized there was a mezzanine level. Upstairs was a gangway and a small office. "There's someone up there," she said.

"Alive?" I resisted the urge to look back at Val.

"They were moving when I noticed them. I think we should check it out before we let Val know."

When we got to the top of the stairs, I could see the person she meant. There was a woman sitting in a chair, her head hanging, hair falling around her face. It looked like she was tied to the chair, her arms were pulled back and she seemed to hang from her shoulders. She moved slightly as she breathed, so I knew she was alive.

We entered the office and Leigh knelt in front of the girl. I held my breath as she tilted the woman's head. It wasn't Emma. She looked nothing like the sketch Val showed me. There was duct tape over her mouth, and bruises that looked like they were a day or two old marred her face.

I felt drained. I didn't realize how much I wanted it to be Emma, to have that search over and done, one way or another.

Leigh was cutting the duct tape around the girl's hands. I didn't want to think about how she was planning to remove the tape from the girl's mouth. Leigh turned to me and nodded her head into the corner. I saw another girl slumped there.

It was Emma, and she wasn't moving.

"It's her," I confirmed as I walked toward the girl. Emma was lying like a broken doll. Her head resting on her shoulder, arms and legs sprawled. I crouched and touched her just under her jaw line. There was a faint beat. I felt tears rise.

"We need a doctor up here." I looked at Leigh as I spoke.

"They are on their way, but we need a sister up here too, I think."

I went to the head of the stairs and called to Val, "Hey, come up here."

She ran up and looked at the first girl then at me.

"No, it's not..." I stepped aside so she could see Emma.

THIRTY-TWO

It all seemed to go quickly after finding Emma.

She regained consciousness as the paramedics checked her over. Val went with her to the hospital, and I told her to take a cab back to the house when she was ready.

Lu and I went to the police station to give our statements. Leigh told us she wouldn't be charging Emma with anything, so we could take her home. They were still trying to sort out why she'd been taken and yet kept alive for so long.

Lu drove me to the marina. I needed to sleep for a week, but I had to make arrangements for Emma to stay with us.

My house was going to be crowded, but it would be fine.

"Charity," Lu said as she dropped me off. "Rest, okay? No new cases for at least a week, right?"

"That sounds great." My bruises were throbbing, my face and ribs were aching, and I couldn't imagine anything better than crawling into bed until I healed. "I'll call you tomorrow."

The weather had cooled and it was windy in the marina. I usually loved the feeling of wind against my skin. Usually it energized me. Today it just sucked the last dregs of energy from my soul.

I could see my front door from the gate and kept my focus clearly on it. I figured Val would be there, and if they had released Emma from the hospital, I'd have two guests.

"Charity," Delores voice broke through my misery. "I'm glad you are home."

"Hi, Delores." I reminded myself of the kindness she'd shown after the break-in and I tried not to sound too miserable. "It's nice to be home."

"Your young friend, Val, was here earlier." I tried to ignore the feeling that she was about to complain.

"Good. I wasn't sure if she was home."

"Well, she isn't. I have to say, she was a nice girl, but I don't think you should bringing so many young women into your home. You won't have a moment's peace with so many teenagers around."

"Oh. Her sister came, too?"

"Well she had another girl with her." Delores pulled her cardigan close, she was feeling the cold too, I guess. "They left with bags an hour ago."

"Thanks for letting me know." I guess they were getting settled, maybe taking out the garbage and getting Emma's stuff. "Anyway, I'll see you tomorrow, Delores, thanks."

I dug for my keys in my purse and opened my door.

It felt wrong.

There was no mess, unlike the last time. It just felt empty. I looked at Val's bedroom. The air mattress was deflating. Her things weren't strewn around. There was a note on the counter. My throat closed around tears before I opened the note.

Charity, thanks for everything. Emma is okay, they had drugged her, but she's fine, nothing addicting. I know I should hang around to say goodbye, but I just can't. I promise we'll be fine. I have some great ideas for businesses. How about Painting by Val - ha ha. You did a good thing finding Emma. Don't worry about us. We will be fine.

The last sentence was underlined twice.

I pictured her writing it. I could hear her giggle as she wrote *ha ha*.

I choked on the first tears and grabbed for Kleenex. I wanted to say goodbye. I wanted to help them get set up.

It took me an hour to cry myself out.

THIRTY-THREE

When the tears stopped, I wandered around the house and finally noticed the world outside.

It was dark, and I saw lights on at Jake's. Great. I needed comfort, and he was very good at comfort and I suddenly missed him for more than just the physical. My heart skipped a beat.

I grabbed my keys and a bottle of wine and ran over to his door. It was unlocked, so I just walked right in.

"Boy, am I glad to see you," I said to the general direction of the kitchen where water was running. "How come you're back so soon?"

"Really? It's nice to be wanted." Not Jake's voice. A nice voice though, warm, and deep.

"Oh, you're not Jake," Miss Originality said.

"Nope." A man walked around the corner of the kitchen, tall, long legs, broad shoulders, blue eyes, blond hair, and a great smile. "He's my nephew. Yeah, I know that look. We're the same age, born three days apart."

"Nice to meet you." I tried not to drool, but it was hard.

"Sorry, you must be Charity." He wiped his hands on a tea towel and reached out to shake mine. "I'm Blake."

His hand was firm, and warm. "Jake and Blake, your mothers had a sense of humor."

"Yup, but they could have called us Thing One and Thing Two so I guess it's not too bad. Shall I open that?" He reached for the bottle of wine, and I let him take it.

"Where's Jake?"

"I'm surprised he hasn't called you."

My heart skipped a beat again, in a bad way. What did Jake have to talk to me about? A lovely compliant actress he had met?

"I've been kind of busy." I patted my pockets. "Phone's at home."

"His part in the movie grew. He'll be there for a couple of months. I'm sure you'll have a message when you get back to your phone."

Phew, that was good news. "Uh huh." I said. He poured two glasses of wine and handed me one of them. "So, you came here to housesit?"

"I needed a place to stay, and Jake said I could stay here."

I clinked my glass with his and gave a silent thanks to Jake for the distraction. "So, you must know so many great stories about him as a kid."

WANT MORE?

Charity and Lu head off to the South of France and face smugglers, corrupt police, and a kidnapping no one seems to care about. Use the QR code to grab a copy of GREED.

Sneak peek on the next page.

If you enjoyed reading Hubris, please consider helping other readers to find the story by leaving a review.

CHAPTER 1

It had been three months since Jake went to Morocco to make a movie. Three months of emails and phone calls, and a growing feeling that I was losing him.

My work as a private investigator hadn't been fascinating since I'd finished with the people traffickers. I'd had a couple of wandering spouse cases. One of them wasn't even wandering. He'd forgotten to tell his wife he was going fishing. I was getting pretty tired of boring cases.

I'd taken the leap into adulthood and decided to stop dabbling in investigating and actually put some effort into my business. Charity Deacon Investigations now had a website. I had a business coach and a five-year plan. But right now, I had a lack of business. When Jake called to say he was given a week off filming and would I like to spend some time with him in Paris, I jumped at the chance.

When I told Lu, she said, "Let's get out of this freaky spring chill and add on a week in the South of France. You'll be better for the break and I'll get a vacation."

We were leaving in six hours.

I had my passport, some euros, and an empty suitcase. And

a pile of clothes on my bed that was too big to fit in the case. I still had time to get a bigger suitcase, but something told me that I would just find more things to bring with me.

I made a pot of coffee to help me think. When I had my mug in hand, I decided that I should make a pile of the essentials; clothes, toiletries and put other stuff to the side.

When I was done, I was staring at the pile of clothes, which might now fit into my suitcase, when the doorbell chimed. Thankful for the interruption, I headed downstairs.

Standing on the finger dock was Delores Markham, neighborhood gossip and rule keeper. I readied myself for some kind of lecture. A quick glance over Delores' shoulder showed me Lu making her way toward us. Unlike me, Lu was looking chic in black and cream. Tall and slim, and perfectly groomed, she always looked elegant. It wasn't just because she was rich, or Asian, there was something cool inside her.

I was tall, but built a little more solidly, and I lived in jeans and tee-shirts. Today, I didn't have to check in the mirror to know I was looking harried and messy.

I looked back at my neighbor and hoped my taste never went to heather and beige outfits. "Come in, Delores," I said, keeping my voice cheerful.

I left the door open so Lu could just walk in. Since gang members broke into my little floating home and trashed it, I had the door set up to lock when it closed. It meant I had to keep a spare key in my car, but I slept better knowing I couldn't accidentally leave the door unlocked.

"Thank you, Charity," Delores said, pulling her cardigan around her as if she was cold. "I understand you are going to France today."

Lu walked in and went straight to the kitchen. "Can I pour you a coffee, Delores?" she asked.

"No, thank you, Lu." Delores smiled as she spoke which kind of put me off kilter.

She had been so nice to me when I got beaten up and came home to find my house a disaster zone. I knew there was a nice Delores in there, an interesting one even. It just seemed she preferred to show the world the judgmental Delores. Or maybe Lu was right, and the judgment was all in my mind.

"Yes, we're off to France. I'm just packing. Is there something I can do for you?" I tried to convey a feeling of urgency without seeming to push her out the door.

"Yes. I would like to ask you a small favor. I have a friend in *Pina sur Midi*. It's a small town on the Mediterranean, near Cassis. Will you be going in that direction?" Delores' voice caught on the last question. This was more than a small favor. I looked a little closer and noticed shadows under her eyes. Delores was worried enough to lose sleep.

I pulled one of the chairs out and asked her to sit. "We'll be close enough to go. What's the favor?" I waited. The tension she wore like a veil didn't shift.

Lu put a box of Kleenex on the table and joined us. At least I wouldn't have to deal with an emotional Delores alone. I hoped she didn't need the Kleenex. I didn't like tears at the best of times, but tears from her would be like the sphinx sobbing.

The words came out in a rush. "Well, my friend, her name is Audrey Wylie, hasn't been in contact for a few days."

"Have you talked to the police?" I figured she was going to ask me to find this Audrey, but I wasn't going to barge into a French police investigation.

"Yes," Delores said. "Of course, I did. The Gendarmes were not very helpful. However, they said they would look into it. A gentleman by the name of Matthieu Durant is in charge of the case."

I could at least try to talk to him, but before I promised, I wanted all the information. "Is it possible that your friend just went away for a few days?"

"She would have told me. Charity, I know there is something wrong. Audrey and I have been friends since we were activists in the sixties. She never lost that drive to fix problems. I know I have grown too old to join protests. But Audrey could never pass up an opportunity to right a wrong. She is quite inspiring."

I ignored Lu's raised eyebrow. I'd tell her what I knew about Delores' history with the Equal Rights Movement later.

"What exactly makes you think something is wrong?" I prompted. Delores was like a lot of my regular clients. The emotions they felt fought with their thinking. Like they could only be logical if they were calm. I was used to prodding until I got what I thought was everything.

"She said she was sure someone was running guns in her town. She told me smuggling was a problem in all the coastal towns, but lately there had been incidents that she thought were more than the normal cargo of marijuana or alcohol. She said that someone might be watching her." Delores dug into her purse and handed me a sheaf of printouts. "Here are all her emails and the information I gave to Mr. Durant. Please, Charity, it would mean a lot if you could make sure the police are taking this seriously."

Who could say no to a scared old lady? It wouldn't hurt to check with the local cops and maybe have a poke around. In fact, doing that would let me write off some of the cost of the trip.

"I can pay you," Delores said, misunderstanding my hesitation.

"No, you don't need to do that. I was just thinking of the best way for us to check. Do you have her address and phone number in here?" I held out the papers.

"Yes, it's on the top page. Thank you, Charity, it means a lot to me." She turned her attention to my home and the worry seemed to slip from her. "I feel like I should be doing something in return. Can I keep an eye on your home while you are gone? And Jake's?"

Despite feeling that I was giving her permission to snoop through my things, I said, "Yes. That would be great. The house sitter I contacted still hasn't gotten back to me, and I don't have time to track her down."

I pulled out my spare keys, Jake's was on there, along with my front door and car. "You don't need to do anything but pick up the mail."

When Delores left, Lu looked at my packing attempt and laughed. "It'll all fit, don't worry." She started rolling the clothes and stuffing them in layers into the case. She looked at the pile of other things I'd set aside. "Why are you bringing your laptop?"

"We might need it for emails or something." *And playing solitaire when I get bored.*

"Leave it here. If we need to be in touch, we'll find an internet cafe."

I started to argue but realized I'd be lugging the laptop with me on the plane, train, and rental car. I decided to go for an unencumbered ride.

CHAPTER 2

When we arrived yesterday, Lu and I had taken the TGV to Avignon and stayed there overnight. Now, after a couple of hours driving on the motorway, we were finishing lunch in a bistro on the outskirts of *Pina sur Midi*. I was already in love with France. Even the suburbs looked like they had been here for a thousand years. It was hot compared to Vancouver, and the sun was welcome. Plane trees were everywhere, lining country roads and standing twisted in the parks we drove by.

Lu put down her coffee cup and called for the bill before saying, "If we keep eating like this, I'll need to start exercising."

Lunch had been mussels and fries, it sounded so much better as *moules and frites*, and a shared dessert to go with the light and refreshing *rosé*. I dug in my purse for the GPS. "Not me. I am going to eat and drink as much as I want. I'll diet when we get back."

We paid the bill. I checked the route to town and lost a little of my holiday buzz. "This looks a bit crazy." I showed Lu the route, which was a tangle of twisting roads and roundabouts. "Let's go to Audrey's first. That way we only have to go into town and find a room, and we don't have to drive out until we leave. Remember the guidebook said to head for the center of town and there would be plenty of hotels."

We followed the GPS to a small house. It looked like a gate-house from a period movie, all pale stone walls, blue Mansard roof, and a heavy wooden door. An ancient wisteria draped itself across a lattice, the lilac cones of blossom swaying in the breeze. There was no doorbell, so I lifted the heavy iron ring and dropped it. The door swung open.

I took a step forward, and Lu grabbed my arm. "Are you sure you should just go in?"

"We could call the cops," I said. "I don't know how long it will take them to get here, though. Delores didn't seem all that impressed with them, and you know how she respects authority."

We tiptoed into the small vestibule, and I stopped so abruptly that Lu almost bowled me over. The inside of the house was a disaster zone. I knew it wasn't a robbery. It reminded me so much of what Jag Chen had done to my home that it must be a warning.

"Charity?" Lu stood with her hand over her mouth. "Should I call the police now?"

"Let's have a look first. If they didn't notice this mess, it's either recent, or they really haven't come by and looked for Audrey. I want to make sure she's not hurt somewhere in that mess before we get stuck answering questions."

The living room was in front of us, so we started there. The couch was ripped, the curtains torn from the rod. Papers were everywhere, some ripped, and some just smashed into a ball and tossed away.

"Be careful you don't trip on this," I said to Lu. I really wanted her to wait in the car, but if she was with me, I wouldn't be worried that something had happened to her. "We'll go through the house once and then call the cops. Or better still, go to them."

The study was buried under a blizzard of paper. Here they'd torn pages from books, and the library shelves had been tossed. The chair and desk were turned over but seemed unbroken.

The powder room was a mess of towels lying in a pool of soap and water. In the dining room, there were a few broken plates on the floor. The only other room downstairs was the kitchen. The damage was confined to a few papers that had drifted from the living room when we opened the door. You have to love the respect the French have for food.

There was no one under the mess. I left Lu downstairs and ran quickly to the second floor, another mess, but no Audrey. I tried to give that a positive interpretation. No body, so Audrey could be okay.

"Do you know if 911 will get the police here?" I called to Lu as I came back down. "This is definitely not just a weekend away kind of thing."

When she didn't answer, I hurried to the living room to see a man in uniform waiting. Lu was standing in a cleared space near the window.

"Madame, I am pleased that you would feel it necessary to inform the gendarmerie that you have entered a place that is clearly a crime scene."

I couldn't believe he was going to pretend we were at fault. "I'm surprised you didn't already know it was a crime scene. This woman has been missing for a week, and you only now come to see what has happened?"

MY ILL-JUDGED comments got us a ride to the station and what was already an hour sitting waiting to be interviewed. It didn't look any different from a Vancouver police station. The walls were painted a color that might have been cream at some point, but now was faded to a gray-yellow that just depressed me.

I must have looked pissed off, because Lu said, "We'll figure it out. Don't worry; it's not your fault we're here. I would kill for a coffee, though."

I thought it was a bit foolish to say you'd kill for anything in a police station, but she was right. And I was getting hungry. Mussels are tasty, but they don't exactly stick to your ribs.

I nudged Lu. "What do you think would happen if we left to get a snack then came back?"

I followed her gaze around the waiting room. Any gendarmes in sight were busy talking to each other, or to a couple of hardened men who were clearly criminals. The other people sitting and waiting were ignoring us. I could almost hear their disdainful 'tourist'.

"We could make a run for it," I said. "Just think, an espresso and pastry. Or maybe a chocolate? Or some ice cream."

"Stop." She smacked my arm, none too gently and laughed. "I don't want to spend the night in jail. And we still need to find a hotel. Try to be helpful when they ask us questions. And let's make it as quick as possible."

"I promise. Hey, maybe we can get a hotel recommendation." I looked at the reception desk. There was a lull in the people hanging out there. There were limits to my patience. I needed to do something. "Be back in a second."

The woman behind the desk was blond and wore little makeup. I wasn't exactly a fashion diva, but she would look ten years younger with a touch of lip gloss and mascara.

"*Oui, Madame.*" she said when I had her attention.

"Do you speak English?" A phrase I'd found very helpful over the last two days.

"Of course," she said in that French way that makes me feel stupid, both for thinking she didn't, and for not speaking French myself. "How can I help you?"

I looked at the nametag she wore, Dominique Girard. "We are waiting to speak to Officer Matthieu Durand. Do you know when he might be available?'

"*Inspecteur* Durand is in a meeting. It may be some time." Most of the time, the French corrected you without attitude; this time the correction came with a thick layer of 'idiot'.

"Do you think it will be okay for us to go and arrange a hotel and then come back?" I didn't mention the fact we'd need a cab to Audrey's where the car was, and we'd stop for a snack, and maybe it would take a couple of hours before we got back.

"It would be better if you waited. I am sure it will not take much longer." She turned back to her computer.

"Then we'll be back in a few minutes." I wasn't asking permission to go get coffee.

She nodded and returned to the computer screen.

"Let's find that coffee," I said when I got back to Lu. "It won't take long."

She gathered up her purse and jacket, and we headed for the door. "I saw a place just down the block."

"*Mesdames* Deacon and Cho?" A male voice called just before we made it outside.

Lu turned and started back. I swore under my breath and joined her.

I assumed this was Matthieu Durand. He was about my height, and blond, with those icy blue eyes that sometimes looked gray. He carried a weariness in his face that was somehow charming. His clothes were rumpled, in a very French chic way.

He looked at us and smiled. It made him hot—not as hot as Jake—but definitely in the top ten of men I knew.

I turned to say something to Lu. My mouth snapped shut. She was blushing, and I saw a shine in her eyes that had been missing since her husband died.

If Matthieu Durand could make my best friend look that alive, then I'd cut him whatever slack he needed.

We followed him to an office. "Please, have a seat. May I get you a coffee?" His voice was a little rough as though he'd been a long-time smoker. But he didn't look like a smoker – unlike what seemed like the majority of people in France.

"That would be pleasant," Lu said before I could answer. "We were just thinking of going for one when you called our names."

Oh, man. Lu had that high tone to her voice, the 'I'm speaking to a guy' voice.

Matthieu called and asked Dominique to bring us coffee. When she brought the tiny espresso cups with a chocolate on the side, I thought she was developing a twitch. She looked at Matthieu like he was a cold beer on a hot day, and at Lu and me as though we were something she'd scraped off her shoes.

As soon as we were alone again, Inspector Durand took out a notebook and started asking questions.

"Have you been in France for long?"

"We arrived yesterday morning." Okay so maybe it wasn't the hardnosed interrogation I expected, but I wasn't planning to give him any information he didn't ask for.

"Ah, you must be experiencing the jet lag." He made a note while he spoke. Then he looked up and focused those great eyes on Lu. "Have you enjoyed your visit?"

Lu smiled at him. "Up to the point where we tried to visit a neighbor's friend, yes. Ms. Wylie seems to have run into some problems."

Good girl. Never let the hormones get in the way of reaching your goals.

"I suppose the break-in happened after you checked on her," she continued.

I watched some expression cross his face. Maybe something was lost in translation, but I could have sworn it was annoyance, and not directed at me for a change.

"Your neighbor?" He pulled a file up on the computer. It didn't come up fast enough apparently because he sighed in annoyance, definitely annoyance. "Ah, yes, Madame Markham. She contacted this department to say she had not heard from Madame Wylie and asked that we visit her home to ensure she was not in danger."

"Yes," I said, joining Durand in his annoyance. "I am interested in what you found. Mrs. Markham had not heard back from your department, despite her repeated emails." I pulled out the sheaf of papers from my purse.

He took them and put them on the edge of his desk. "There have been other priorities. We were able only today to visit Madame Wylie's home."

I bit my tongue. It wouldn't help for me to say they wouldn't have even come today if some nosy neighbor hadn't ratted us out.

"Then it is fortunate that we were also able to visit today," Lu said. "Perhaps you would have had other priorities if we hadn't seen the mess. I assure you we were about to call the police ourselves. I wonder if any of her neighbors were as vigilant on the day the break-in happened."

I totally had to learn that. If I had said the same thing, it would have made things worse. Lu managed to bring a smile to Inspector Durand's face. Maybe the batting of her eyes made the difference.

"Yes, it is fortunate, as you say," he said.

I decided to ride the wave of good feeling. "Inspector

Durand, can you tell us anything that we can pass on to Mrs. Markham. She is very worried."

"Please, call me Matthieu. *Inspecteur* is not a rank in the gendarmerie." He answered my question but looked at Lu the entire time.

I wondered if Dominique thought that telling us a bogus rank would make us look stupid. I guess being on a first name basis was a good sign, though. "Fine, Matthieu, and the information?"

Matthieu finally turned to me. He straightened up and seemed to pull a professional coat on. "We have nothing more than you found. I am going to assume you did not do the damage and so, you are free to go. If you would like to leave your information, I will provide you with an update when we do."

So, suddenly we were all business. "We will stay in town until we have information. Can you recommend a hotel?"

He was about to answer – I wasn't sure if it would be a huffy 'I am not a tourist bureau' or a recommendation – when the door to the office opened behind us. I turned to see a much older man with an immaculate uniform on. It contrasted with the rumpled look Matthieu sported.

"Lieutenant Durand, when you are finished, you are needed in the Colonel's office." I'm not sure why he spoke English, but it seemed like he wanted us to know he was important.

"I will be some time, still, Sargent. *S'il vous plait, fermez la porte.*" I could have sworn that we had been dismissed a minute ago. Perhaps we were and he had other work he needed to do.

Matthieu turned back to Lu. "Now, *Mesdames*, I can recommend a hotel. But, first, I believe your car remains at Madame Wylie's home. Perhaps I can drive you there?"

"Thank you," Lu said. "I'm sure you are far too busy to drive us around." She stood as she spoke and smoothed her capris.

"But perhaps we can revisit the house and you can explain to me what you have discovered – if anything." He shut down the computer and gestured for us to leave. "And you can tell me why it is your neighbor was so sure that her friend was in danger."

He led us to the garage where we climbed into what was obviously his personal vehicle, a beaten-up Renault. I flicked a glance at Lu and then jumped into the back seat.

As we were leaving, a uniformed gendarme strode forward, hand raised to stop the car, but Matthieu stepped on the gas a little and gave a cheerful wave as though he didn't realize they wanted him to stop.

If you want to know more, use the QR code to check out GREED.

FREE EBOOK

Claim your copy of Buying Into Death when you use the QR code to sign up for my newsletter and follow Charity as she solves her fastest case yet!

ALSO BY P A WILSON

For more books by P A Wilson

Use the QR code below or go to pawilson.ca

ABOUT THE AUTHOR

Perry Wilson is a Canadian author based in Vancouver, BC who has big ideas and an itch to tell stories. Having spent some time on university, a career, and life in general, she returned to writing in 2008 and hasn't looked back since (well, maybe a little, but only while parallel parking).

She is a member of the Vancouver Writers Social Group, The Royal City Literary Arts Society, and The Surrey Writing Workshop. Perry has self-published several novels. She writes the Madeline Journeys, a fantasy series about a high-powered lawyer who finds herself trapped in a magical world, the Quinn Larson Quests, which follows the adventures of a wizard named Quinn who must contend with volatile fae in the heart of Vancouver, and the Charity Deacon Investigations, a mystery thriller series about a private eye who tends to fall into serious trouble with her cases, and The Riverton Romances, a series based in a small town in Oregon, one of her favorite states. Her stand-alone novels are Breaking the Bonds, Closing the Circle, and The Dragon at The Edge of The Map.

For more information
www.pawilson.ca
pawilson@pawilson.ca

ACKNOWLEDGMENTS

People think that the process of writing is solitary. That's not the case for me. I have help from so many people it would be hard to acknowledge everyone, but I'll give it a try.

The support and inspiration I get from my writer's groups is incalculable. The Vancouver Writers Social Group opens my mind to other ways of telling a story. The Royal City Literary Arts Society gives me the opportunity to meet and share with other writers who have more knowledge than I do. The Other 11 Months group is where I learn about getting the words on the page. And my critique group who helps me find the best parts of the story I want to tell. Thanks to all of the members of these great groups.

Last of all, but definitely a huge part of the process, my beta readers. These are the people who love stories and are willing, and more than able, to tell me if my finished story is ready for you, my readers.